CW00858438

Tiara

Tiara

John Reinhard Dizon

Published 2016 by Creativia
Book design by Creativia (www.creativia.org)
Cover Design by http://www.thecovercollection.com/

Other Books by John Reinhard Dizon

- *Cyclops*

- *Destroyer (Abaddon)*

- *Generations*

- *Penny Flame*

- *Stxeamtown*

- *The Bat: An Existential Fable*

- *The Fury*

- *The Standard*

- *Wolf Man*

- *Wolfsangel*

Crown of thorns upon my brow
Your tiara my affliction
Its diamonds trickle into my eyes
I've given all carrying your cross
Sacrificed for your noble cause
And now I tire before the night
Blinded by the light
Blinded by your beauty
Just as you've blinded mine
—Princess Jennifer of Edinburgh (2013)

Chapter One

Her mother, Lenore of Scotland, taught her that life was all about choices. Life provided opportunities for everyone, from the rich to the poor, and choices determined one's path in life. Jennifer Mac Manus believed she had a special destiny, a calling to protect and defend the rights of the people of the United Kingdom. As a child she was always the first to volunteer for charity events, the look of joy in the eyes of the unfortunate making the holidays truly special. She chose the happiness of others over the pageantry of the aristocracy, and the humility of the young princess was not overlooked by her people or the world press.

When she entered high school, she became even more involved in humanitarian causes. Poverty, unemployment and women's issues were her main concerns, and she wrote essays and made public appearances whenever possible to promote her agendas. Many of her works were published in newspapers and magazines around the world, and the young scholar was acclaimed by humanitarian groups the world over for her tireless efforts.

Her celebrity was not lost on members of the British monarchy. Prince Conrad of England had become infatuated by the beautiful girl's looks as well as her intelligence and charisma. Though he was nine years her senior, he proposed marriage to her and she readily accepted. She was smitten by the dapper though homely-looking man, knowing that marrying into the Royal Family would be a life-changing event for her. The wedding made headlines around the world, and it appeared to be made in heaven.

Yet the fissures began to appear when the tabloids started rumors that Conrad was still making overtures to his ex-girlfriend, Lady Sarah Hepburn. The Prince vehemently denied it, though his personal life suffered another trauma soon afterward. His great-uncle, Lord Layton, was killed in an Irish Republican Army bombing attack in London. A reporter overheard a grieving Conrad referring to the Irish as 'pigs' at the funeral. It created a scandal that was exacerbated by Lady Hepburn's personal attempts to console the Prince. Jennifer made a public statement disclaiming any animosity towards the Irish by the Royal Family, which was perceived as much as a rebuke to Conrad as a reaction to the controversy surrounding the royal couple. Her efforts to protect and defend her husband was seen as just another of her noble causes.

The Prince's inferiority complex was near-legendary. He tried to make up for his less-than-average looks and his undeserved privilege by establishing a reputation as a ladies' man and dabbling in extreme sports. Though he distanced himself from Lady Hepburn, he was seen with other women at London nightspots and thrilled the media with attempts at hang-gliding and skydiving. It was not long before the unthinkable happened, and Conrad was killed in a speedboat accident that left the Royal Family and the United Kingdom in shock and grief.

Jennifer began devoting her efforts to mending relations with the Irish nation, which had been caught up in a mortal struggle between Loyalists and Republicans in Northern Ireland for nearly half a century. She began meeting with both sides in an effort to bring them together for peace talks in ending the Troubles at last. At first she was denounced as a do-gooder and a meddler, but those who met her began to realize her intentions were sincere. She immersed herself in research on the conflict and soon impressed representatives on both sides with her acumen. Eventually she was accepted as a legitimate mediator and was soon engaged in phone talks with the American President in the international peace effort.

The turning point came when representatives of the outlawed Irish Republican Army were invited to negotiations along with their political branch, Sinn Fein. They would be scheduled to meet with Loyalist emissaries as well as a contingency from the British Government led by Princess Jennifer. It would set a precedent in recognizing the IRA as a combatant force instead of a terrorist group, which would be a breakthrough in securing prisoners' rights and establishing their legitimacy as a military organization.

It was met with outrage by Loyalists throughout Northern Ireland, whose hardline policy defined the IRA as a criminal gang dedicated to the overthrow of the Ulster government. They threatened to boycott the peace talks and hinted at violent reprisals against Republican sympathizers. Militant groups such as the Ulster Defense Association awaited the go-ahead from their political counterparts, welcoming the opportunity to strike back at the hated IRA after chafing under the restrictions of the recent cease-fire. The whole world watched and waited as the next step towards peace in Northern Ireland had yet to be taken.

"I'm against this sitdown, your Highness," Lord Scott Lipscomb, Jennifer's most trusted advisor, remained adamant as they approached the weekend of the peace negotiations at Stormont Castle in East Belfast. They met at Holyrood Palace in Edinburgh, where Jennifer began spending more time after Conrad's death to lend her aura of prestige to the Scottish monarchy. "The possibilities of disaster are endless. It is almost as if we're trying to ride a two-headed mule. Neither side seems willing to budge despite the fact that the Empire, the European Union and the United States are all doing everything in their power to make this happen. The crux of the argument is that we are legitimizing these IRA gangsters in the eyes of the world by inviting them to the table. There are rumors of the meeting itself being a target of a terror attack by extremists on both sides. I don't think anyone would blame you for missing this meeting."

"That's impossible, Scott," Jennifer insisted. She was a lovely woman at 5'6", 130 pounds, with long blonde hair and emerald eyes, a generous bosom and an hourglass figure. "We were the ones who set this meeting up. How could we possibly walk away after getting both sides to give us their commitment? Not showing up is telling the whole world we don't trust either side."

"If anything were to happen, it would entirely destroy the peace talks as well as cause irreparable damage to the Royal Family. Lord Layton was killed just a couple of years ago by terrorists, and our people are just recovering from the loss of the Prince. How could you expect us to bear yet another catastrophe if you were attacked by a gang of murderers?"

"We're going to be going around and around with this, and it's not going to accomplish anything. I think if we spent more time coordinating the event rather than planning to avoid it, we can ensure an even greater success. Why not look into having some special events for children and senior citizens from the Catholic and Protestant communities? Surely even the most hardcore extremists have a heart for their own children and the elderly. We can also invite church leaders from both sides to help us plan some events. If we use our imagination and put some effort into it, we can make all kinds of things happen."

"These people don't give a damn about church or religion, it's never been about that. It's about the economy and political power. The Catholics are tired of being treated like foreigners in their own country, and the Protestants think we're going to abandon them to the Republican agenda and allow them to be absorbed into the Irish state. Both sides are like children frightened of being turned out into the cold."

"They are our children, aren't they?" Jennifer insisted. "They're part of our family, and they will be treated as such. We have a responsibility to both sides, and history will be our judge if we do not take this opportunity to bring peace to Ulster at last."

"I hope you're right, Your Highness. I certainly hope you're right."

* * *

Berlin Mansfield would long wonder when his love affair with Jennifer Mac Manus began, or what it was that first enticed him. Was it the beauty of her publicity photos, the charisma and personality she exuded during her speeches, or the hint of the woman she was away from the cameras? He could never know for sure. What he did know was that he grew more fascinated as time passed, and the more he heard about her the more he wanted to meet her. When he was given an offer to take a contract to kill her, he decided it would be a perfect opportunity for their paths to cross at last.

"One hundred million?" the Al Qaeda representative asked in disbelief as Mansfield made his bid for the job. "Surely you jest. The Sheik's entire fortune is estimated at $300 million. Even if we asked you to kill the President of the United States I do not think you would be offered that kind of money."

"I'm quite certain that you would," Mansfield fixed his steely-eyed gaze on his host. They were meeting at Rules Restaurant on Maiden Lane in the Covent Garden district of London where they enjoyed a sumptuous dinner of Belted Galloway beef before getting down to business. Four Muslim gunmen stood watch around the rear booth as the terrorists discussed terms that evening. "Only the Americans would wipe you off the face of the earth if I did such a work for you. The Sheik is becoming quite the public figure these days. An interview on ABC News, following his ongoing discussions on the airwaves with Al-Jazeera. Certainly he realizes the worst thing that can happen to someone in this business is to be recognized, much less become a celebrity. If I killed the President for you, they would drop a nuclear bomb anywhere any of you was hiding."

"You are the most wanted man on the planet next to the Sheik," the Arab chuckled. "We would think you are quite a public figure in your own right."

"That may be," Mansfield shrugged. "Yet even you don't know what I look like."

"Of course," the Arab smiled softly. "The Man of a Thousand Faces. You are so right, my friend. The nations of the world search for a man they cannot even identify."

"You know, I don't want to offend the Sheik. I don't want him to think that I am highballing him, or overpricing myself to get out of the job. Can you get him on the phone and see if he'll go for a better price?" Mansfield asked in an American accent. He took great pleasure in having those he met return to their superiors with completely different reports about the man they expected to meet.

"That is not possible, my friend. You know that. How much are we talking about?"

"Ninety million. I will kill her for ninety million."

"My dear Mansfield," the Arab looked down at his cup of espresso ruefully. "We are discussing the Princess of Edinburgh. If we asked you to kill both Elizabeth and the Queen Mother we might consider it. This woman is worth no more than ten million at the most, and for that I would have to get approval from the Sheik."

"I've developed a gas similar to the Sarin compound," Mansfield disclosed, taking a sip of his Moet et Chandon champagne. "It is entirely odorless and contains the same corrosives, only I've added a flammable component that can only be set off by another gaseous element. My team would release the gas near where the Princess was situated by means of a device that would spread the chemical along a twenty-yard radius. Once the secondary device was activated, her lungs along with everyone else's, and everything within contact, would explode in flames that would be impossible to extinguish for the first thirty seconds of combustion."

"Sell us the formula," the Arab insisted. "We will do the job ourselves with such a weapon. Name your price for this gas of yours."

"Therein lies the problem. If you had the gas you wouldn't need me."

"Ten million for the job, and twenty million for the formula. I will transfer the funds to your Swiss account immediately."

"My friend, as the Americans say, you're not even in the ballpark," Mansfield swallowed the dregs in his glass and rose to his feet. "Tell the Sheik how much I need, have him get back to me. You know how it works. If he considers seventy mil perhaps we can discuss this."

"It has been an honor to meet you," the Arab rose to shake his hand.

"Keep the faith," Mansfield hugged him. "We are all within a heartbeat of meeting Allah."

Mansfield left the restaurant, going to his BMW parked across the lot from the Arabs' Mercedes Benz. He quickly popped the trunk and pulled out a magnetic device, rushing over to the Arabs' vehicle and placing it on its underside. He darted back to his car and climbed inside, gunning the engine and cruising off the lot to a parking spot on the opposite side of the street. He was able to see the Mercedes from the rear view mirror as he activated the remote control device in the case on the seat beside him.

His logic was that Al Qaeda had refused to meet his price, making it seem as if Osama Bin Laden was their only source of financing, which he knew was a falsehood. Although he had overbid the job as he did not intend to kill the Princess, this was no longer the issue. Since they had tipped their hand, now Mansfield was a potential liability as he had knowledge of a possible attempt on her life. One of the extremists on the upper echelon might decide that Mansfield, in refusing to assist in the mission and knew of its existence, was an enemy of Allah who must be destroyed.

He waited until the five men exited the restaurant and got in the car. He figured that Al Qaeda would suspect either the Mossad or MI6 had discovered the presence of the terrorists and ordered the assassination. In either case, the name of Berlin Mansfield would most likely not come up as a possible suspect.

He opened the window and held the detonator out, pressing the button as the Mercedes Benz exploded with a deafening roar. He then put it back in its case and drove a block before putting it in a small sack and tossing it into a trash barrel on a street corner. He then headed back to his room at Claridge's in the Mayfair district, switching on the radio until he found a classical station to help lighten his mood.

Maybe Al Qaeda would be more accommodating in future.

* * *

The next morning, Jon Stevens and Slash Scimitar made their way along Great Eastern Street on the East End en route to the Hoxton Hotel. It was located in a trendier area of town frequented by young people, students and artists. The two men were somewhat surprised that their host had selected a place like this for an overnight stay, yet they also realized it was the least likely place someone like him would be found.

Fritz Hammer was a CIA legend, a Special Forces Captain in Vietnam who had over two hundred registered kills to his credit. He was sent to Iraq to direct traffic during Operation Desert Shield, taking down the remnants of Saddam Hussein's Republican Guard in the cleanup operations after the invasion. He then was sent to Serbia where he worked alongside militia forces loyal to the defunct Yugoslavian government before the country collapsed under civil war. He met Jon and Slash there, and sponsored their transfer to the Paramilitary Division where they were ranked among its top operatives. Hammer needed a favor and the men were glad to help.

"I'm sure you fellows are up to speed on the bombing last night," Fritz said as he switched on the BBC broadcast on TV though muting the volume. Hammer walked around with a cane after suffering a hip injury during the Fall of Saigon. It did nothing to affect his career though he was notoriously grumpy on cold, humid days such as this.

"Yes sir, they mentioned that at least one of the victims was a known Al Qaeda operative," Jon replied. He was an auburn-haired, athletically built man with lively green eyes and a quick smile. He was often mistaken for an artist or a student and would never be suspected of being one of the CIA's most accomplished assassins and saboteurs. Slash, a tall, lanky man with a swarthy look, was just as affable and every bit Jon's equal on the field.

"MI6 had a different take on how that went down," Fritz replied. He was six feet tall with a blond crewcut and blue eyes, having reached 210 pounds after leaving the service though one could see it was solid muscle. "Their informants in Lebanon got word that they had been in contact with Berlin Mansfield to discuss a joint project. They don't know who it was that made the Al Qaeda agents, and of course everyone's denying any involvement. The overriding concern now is Mansfield. MI6 is on full alert, trying to determine whether Mansfield is in-country."

"Berlin Mansfield," Jon glanced over at Slash as they sat on armchairs facing Hammer, who was propped against the headboard of the comfortable double bed. "That's some heavy shit. What do they figure him for, blowing up Big Ben? London Bridge?"

"We have no idea. What we are concerned with is the upcoming peace negotiations scheduled at the Hotel Europa this weekend. The entire thing is a train wreck waiting to happen, but it's gone too far to call off. Some of the biggest IRA godfathers in Northern Ireland are scheduled to be there, as well as the top Unionist leaders and delegates from Parliament. Death threats were coming from everywhere, but everyone finally realizes that an attack on one will be an attack on all. Even so, an international terrorist organization like Al Qaeda or someone like Mansfield wouldn't be concerned by any such repercussions."

"Why would they be sticking their nose into something like that?" Slash wondered.

"The IRA's been doing business with the PLO[1] for a number of years now. A peace agreement would result in a major loss of revenue. Plus an attack by Al Qaeda against the UK could easily be construed as a blow against British imperialism."

"Makes sense. Do we get tickets to the ball?"

"I want you guys to conduct surveillance outside the hotel. There will be a small security detachment in place to protect Princess Jennifer and the delegates, but the police and MI6 will not be out in force because they don't want to scare off the IRA representatives. The reasoning is that MI6, the Constabulary and everyone else would be using the occasion to update their databases. Everyone knows that the IRA will be sending their own bodyguards along with their spokesmen, so for all attempts and purposes they'll be providing security for everyone."

"Who in hell dreamed all this up?"

"Who knows. You can be sure the Brits'll have personnel on standby for ready deployment in case of emergency, but they'll be keeping the immediate vicinity clear to allay suspicion of a double-cross. I'll bet the police would probably have warrants on half the delegates if they had their way out there. Princess Jennifer and her people gave their word, and the Brits'll have to abide by it."

---

1. Palestine Liberation Organization

"So how are we gonna get away with loitering on the street?"

"You two'll be hanging out at the Crown Bar across the street. Keep your eyes open, find a spot by the window, go on outside for a smoke and take a little stroll. You two have been on these kinds of assignments as many times as anyone else in the Company. You know exactly what to look for. You see anyone looking like they're setting up shop you'll move in, intercept their operatives and abort the operation."

"Will we be carrying?"

".22 caliber pistols at best. In the event there are any British agents in the Crown Bar, I wouldn't want them putting the make on you and having you intercepted. You have to understand, this war has been going on for a long time. Lots of British agents, soldiers and cops have seen close friends go six feet under during this conflict. Everyone realizes that having IRA men walking down Great Victoria Street is going to be like parading canaries before a row of alley cats. The UDA[2] would love to plant a car bomb in front of the hotel if it weren't for the fact that some of their top guys'll be inside. We can't prepare for everything, but having you two out near the front of the place will provide some assurance."

"What's the Company's interest here?"

"In case you hadn't noticed, the President is Irish-American. There's nothing he'd want more than to have his name associated with a peace agreement in Northern Ireland. There's even rumors he's planning to invite Gerry Adams and Martin McGuinness to the White House. If anything were to go down and you two kept it from happening, rest assured you'd probably end up with executive jobs in Langley for the rest of your careers."

"Like you?"

"That's it. Get out."

"Good seeing you again."

"Give my best to the Princess."

"Sure will."

* * *

In the fishing village of Dundalk just outside the Irish border, Mike O'Beirne had made arrangements to meet with a special guest. O'Beirne was one of the

2. Ulster Defense Association

most important IRA godfathers in Ulster, and was generally considered to be semi-retired though highly respected by the Army Councils in each major city. He had been invited as one of the IRA delegates at the meeting at the Hotel Europa, and was contacted shortly thereafter by this visitor.

Despite the fact the man came alone, Mike had three cars of four-man fire teams posted around the property. When they found out who was visiting O'Beirne they were just as alarmed as he was, yet would not think of leaving the venerated leader to his own devices. They came armed to the teeth and stared around the countryside, wondering what contingencies the visitor might have made in ensuring his own security.

"So what brings you down here to Dundalk?" Mike asked, lighting his pipe as they sat in front of his fireplace in the stately cottage. They were both comfortable on the overstuffed recliners in the traditionally furnished living room.

"Business and pleasure," Berlin Mansfield smiled. O'Beirne would have never recognized him from the last time they met. He was no more recognizable then than he was the time before that. Mike's red hair had grayed over the past ten years, and he had wrinkled considerably as a result of the tension caused by the Troubles. He remembered Mansfield from a bombing in London, and had briefly spent time with him as the operation progressed. He hardly considered Mansfield an acquaintance, and was more than surprised when Berlin called to arrange a visit.

"What pleasure could there be in this business of ours?" Mike wondered.

"You know my father was from Belfast. My roots are here."

"Aye, but you were born in that splendid city you were named after. This business is your trade. Those of us involved in our struggle were forced into it."

"Come now, Mike. There are more than a few who have profited well from it. You didn't pay for this lovely abode with a laborer's pension."

"Laborers earn their keep. Your name's appeared in *Forbes Magazine* alongside those of Pablo Escobar and Osama Bin Laden."

"Sometimes people pay me to stay out of their business. Did you wonder what that car bomb in London was about the other night?"

"And why would I be privy to that information?"

"You seem kind of defensive, and not all too friendly. Is there something that has offended you?"

"You know, I've only met you once in my life. Since then you've become the second most wanted man alive. You can't blame me for being a bit tentative here."

"Relax. Please," Mansfield smiled. "I come here as a friend, I assure you. I would have you tell your men outside that I came alone, but I wouldn't want them to take the situation for granted."

"Well, friend, what brings you here, if I may be so direct?"

"I was offered a contract to kill the Princess of Edinburgh for thirty million dollars."

"Shit," Mike exhaled. "So did you take it?"

"There were complications. I never showed up at the meeting at the restaurant. That doesn't mean the threat no longer exists. I want to provide security for you and your men at the Europa on Friday."

"There's no way. We couldn't afford you ten years ago."

"I'm going to do the work free of charge."

"And why would you want to do that? Why wouldn't I think you're just looking for a chance to get close to the Princess?"

"Well, that is the reason. I want to meet her."

"What?" Mike squinted. "Berlin, please. If you were me, what would you be thinking right now?"

"Probably the same thing you are. I ask that you hear me out. I find the woman fascinating. I believe in what she's doing, and I believe she can succeed. I was not happy to find out that Al Qaeda had evil intentions towards her, but in retrospect I realized there may be many others in line to take her out of the picture. Many of my business connections see her as the face of British imperialism. She represents the Empire. She is putting her imprimatur on this agreement on behalf of the authority that has subjugated the Irish people for centuries. Killing her not only strikes a blow against the Empire, but ends the negotiation entirely. Do you realize there are many people who do not want to see a peaceful end to your struggle?"

"Nobody even knows what you look like. I don't know what you look like. Who's going to know that you're part of the security force? If the Brits had a clue that you were among us, all bets would be off. They would come in and arrest you as if you were Bin Laden himself."

"I'll take care of the details. You just give me a time and place, and I'll meet up with your entourage on the way to the hotel."

"No tricks, Berlin," Mike rose to shake hands as Mansfield took his leave. "If anything happens to her, you'll pay the price. My people as well as our Irish community have too much at stake here."

"Rest assured that those in the terror community will want no part in this once I've spread the word. Come Friday, I'll be the best friend you could have."

Mike O'Beirne and his men watched Berlin Mansfield's BMW drive off. They realized they were among the few people in the world who had laid eyes on the man since he became the second most wanted fugitive on the planet.

* * *

Baxter Cody had chosen the military as an alternative to prison before Operation Desert Storm, and had served in Iraq with the Special Air Service. He was decorated for valor and returned to the streets of Belfast as a war hero. Only he exchanged one war for another in doing so, volunteering his services as a squad leader in C Company of the 3rd Battalion under UDA godfather Eddie "The Bull" Doherty. The conflict began slowly and escalated accordingly. Cody saw the struggle as a military campaign, and resented the battalion being run like a street gang. Doherty did his best to keep his lieutenants from treating Cody and his men as a pack of boy scouts, while his top gun Delmore Merrick could see trouble ahead.

Both Doherty and Cody saw major problems ahead if the peace agreement went into effect, but for different reasons. Doherty realized that if the police campaign against the IRA came to an end, they might well refocus their efforts in a crackdown against the UDA's street operations. Their multimillion-dollar drug, loansharking, extortion and gambling rackets would all be at risk. Alternately, Cody saw the nightmare of Ulster seceding from the UK as a distinct possibility. He and others like him would fight a civil war before that happened.

Cody had begun to develop his reading and writing skills while in the military, and did considerable study on the history of the UK. He was proud of his heritage as a citizen of the Empire and his Scots-Irish ancestry. He began writing reports on the sociopolitical situation in Northern Ireland and submitting them to Merrick, who dutifully handed them over to Doherty. Eddie tossed them into a drawer in his office at the Orange Order Lodge on Newtownards Road which he used as his unofficial headquarters. After a few months there were over a dozen reports that had gone unread and forgotten.

He arrived at the Lodge on Thursday night and demanded a meeting with Doherty. Merrick knew that Doherty was in the middle of negotiations with a couple of visitors from the London Mob. They had been sent by Billy Belfast to finalize a deal on a million-pound heroin shipment en route from England to Ulster. The security arrangements for Princess Jennifer's visit was forcing the Mob to reroute the shipment from London to Larne instead of Belfast. Cody's squad was one of Doherty's top smuggling team, and his visit could not come at a better time.

"Just in time, my boy," Doherty was in a gregarious mood as he entertained the London gangsters, surrounded by four of his own top gunmen. The meeting had ended and they were enjoying drinks and sandwiches before heading downtown for some carousing. "I was going to have Delmore give you a call to make sure you'll be available next week for that project we discussed."

"Yes, sir," Cody stood at ease, stepping forth long enough to place yet another report on the table before Doherty. "I wanted to make sure that you were aware that my squad is on standby for the upcoming event at the Hotel Europa and ready to move forward with our mission."

"Mission?" Doherty lit a cigar, the white-haired gangster squinting at Merrick. "What mission is that?"

"He's been sending us reports almost every other week," Merrick shook his head. "I've been putting them in the top right hand drawer of your desk. He's been giving up updates on the political situation in Ulster and how the peace negotiations are disrupting our way of life here in Belfast. He's got a lot of good ideas on how to derail the entire process. Maybe you should start paying attention before something gets signed this weekend that you're not going to like."

"You see that?" Doherty gestured at Cody, smiling at the London hoods. "This is an example of the kind of kids we've got coming up the ranks these days. Not only is he one of my best smugglers, but he knows what the hell's going on in the world. He knows what those ninnies in Stormont are up to, he knows what the politicians in London are planning, and he knows what needs to be done to toss their whole plan upside down. These kids are the future of our organization, make no mistake about it."

"Sir, the discussions at the Hotel Europa are scheduled to begin tomorrow night. I've come to make sure that we've got your blessings and the go-ahead to commence our own operations once everything's in place."

"What operations are those?" Doherty wondered.

"Sir, considering of the nature of our operation, I regret not being able to discuss the details in public. I can assure you that we have gone over all the contingencies and remain highly confident that our plan will succeed. We will not only disrupt the conference but place the blame for our actions directly at the doorstep of our Republican enemies. Rest assured that they will be under greater pressure from the authorities than ever before."

"Well, that sounds like a good deal to me," Doherty grinned. "As long as you and your men will be able to help us make that delivery from Larne that we discussed. You go ahead and run your errand as long as you be sure and tend to mine."

"Thank you, sir," Cody saluted before taking his leave.

"Have you even taken a look at his reports?" Merrick asked as the other gangsters laughed and shook their heads.

"Sure, I'm looking at it," Doherty chuckled. With that, he tossed one of the most incriminating documents in recent Ulster history into a nearby trash can.

Chapter Two

The Grand Ballroom of the Hastings Hotel Europa was one of the most elegant banquet facilities in downtown Belfast. Its crystal chandeliers were set within the golden ceilings, its matching gold curtains draped along the dais where candelabras highlighted the impeccably-set tables across the spacious room. The staff lined up along the walls, quick to assist and serve the guests as they arrived for the historic event. The Sinn Fein delegates looked about apprehensively, identifying themselves as such though a large number were actually staff members of IRA battalions throughout Ulster. They were accompanied by hard-faced bodyguards who would rely on the guarantees of their hosts that they would not have to fight their way out of this meeting.

A band called the Emerald Strings played classical music until the ceremonies began, after which another group called the Menu took over with a repertoire of modern pop tunes. The master of ceremonies opened that segment with greetings and introductions of the delegates, followed by short speeches by the Northern Ireland Secretary of State, an Ulster Unionist leader and the Assembly Group Leader of Sinn Fein. The Princess of Edinburgh was the featured speaker, and she thanked everyone for coming in guaranteeing that this weekend would be a milestone event in heading towards the Peace Agreement scheduled for 1998.

The guests were treated to Irish Smoked Salmon appetizers, and the cocktail bars remained open as the music resumed after the speeches had ended. The negotiations were set to begin at noon tomorrow in the Dublin Room on the second floor. The weekend would end with a luncheon at noon on Sunday featuring a religious service to honor God and those who had contributed to the peace process. This evening would allow the delegates to mingle on a casual basis and prepare them for the formal discussions ahead.

Princess Jennifer received a long line of visitors, most of whom had come by to pay their respect and thank her for the invitation. She was resplendent in a dark green evening gown that offset her golden hair, and an 18-karat Buccellati leaf ensemble including matching earrings. The men were dazzled by her beauty and were delighted to pose for pictures as the opportunity presented itself.

"May I have this dance?"

Jennifer was taken aback by the unexpected request, and did a double-take at the six foot, 185-pound man with the athletic build whose longish blond hair framed a ruggedly handsome face accentuated by his piercing blue eyes and pouting lips. He had a powerful aura that was far different than the demeanor of the gangsters and the career politicians. This was not bravado, this was a dragonslayer of ages past who had come to meet a Princess.

"Why, certainly," she hesitated for a microsecond. She certainly was not prepared to dance, but she had lived her life unaffected by protocol or procedure and would not be so restricted now. She took the black-suited man's arm and soon the crowd gave way as they stole the spotlight to the bossa nova tune of "The Look of Love". They surprised each other as they stepped into a bossa nova blues sequence that neither had trouble adapting to.

"What in hell is he doing?" the commander of the IRA's South Armagh Brigade sidled over to Mike O'Beirne as the guests at the Sinn Fein tables stared in amazement. "What in hell has he been drinking? Has he lost his mind? There're cameras all over this feckin' place."

"Some men have a death wish, I suppose. There also those who feel they have no limits and live accordingly. He said he came here to meet her, and now he's gotten his wish."

Undercover MI6 agents furtively instructed cameramen to get pictures of the couple, though the dashing man seemed entirely unconcerned by all the attention.

"You're a wonderful dancer," Jennifer beamed as she danced like never before. He had professional moves and glided with her across the floor as if they were walking on air. "Tell me your name."

"My name is Jim Jones," he had a hint of a German accent. "I'm with the Sinn Fein delegation from West Belfast. I had a dream of dancing with a beautiful princess since I was a young boy. You've fulfilled a childhood wish."

"You know, they're going to get me for this, but I want to request one more. Let's go by the bandstand."

Many in the audience stood in applause, though the entire ballroom watched in fascination as the couple remained on the floor for another bossa nova tune, "The Girl from Ipanema". This time they earned a rousing ovation and the cheers of some of the streetwise attendees as they warmed up to the dance, performing more flawlessly than at first. Jim Jones escorted her back to the dais and kissed her hand before returning to his table.

"Colonel, I've got pictures ready to transmit," one of the MI6 agents hurried out to the outside lobby to a quiet corner near a service entrance. "We got some decent face shots, but we couldn't get too close because the IRA suspects were on high alert. Some of them were restrained by their own people from confronting the hotel's photography crew."

"All right, send them," Colonel Mark O'Shaughnessy ordered. He was aloft in a Griffin HAR2, the military helicopter flying up and down the River Lagan that coursed through the Belfast City area. O'Shaughnessy was a living legend in the SAS, held in the same esteem as Fritz Hammer with the CIA. He had earned his bones in Northern Ireland though also serving in Africa, Iraq and Serbia in the 90's. He was the highest ranking officer in the Ulster theatre of operations and had particular interest in this event.

He knew that Berlin Mansfield had been suspected of involvement in the restaurant bombing last weekend. He had long dreamed of meeting Mansfield on the field and ending his career. He had just missed Mansfield at the beginning of their careers during the Beirut Bombing of 1983. He had tracked the Mansfield Gang down in Rwanda in 1994 where they were playing both sides of the fence in the Hutu-Tutsi race wars for blood diamonds. They escaped to Serbia in 1995 where they were suspected of trafficking human organs for the Chinese. It was rumored that Mansfield was offering his mercenary services for the Second Congo War in progress. Taking down Mansfield would be the highlight of his own unparalleled career. He was certain Mansfield was here but could not believe he was actually at the Hotel Europa.

"This is O'Shaughnessy," he called Scotland Yard from the chopper, which was equipped with some of the most sophisticated communication equipment on the planet. "I'm sending along some images taken minute ago at the Europa in Belfast. I want FFI[1] run on this, and copies sent to SIS[2]. I need positive ID on this individual and I want the Chief to be prepared to authorize an arrest pending confirmation."

"Who's the person of interest?"

"The Golden Terror."

"The Prime Minister's declared the activity off-limits, but I'll see what we can do."

O'Shaughnessy's well-known temper worsened as the Griffin soared above the Belfast night sky. He could not believe they were protecting these scoundrels, even if they were providing them with immunity during this event. They had an invaluable opportunity to update their information, and if Mansfield was in the hotel there must be a way to circumvent these restrictions. If Bin Laden himself showed up there would have been no qualms over making an arrest. O'Shaughnessy could not see how this was any different.

"Sir, the reports are coming back negative."

"What? Then who the hell is this fellow?"

"Unknown, sir. We've got no record of him. Is there any way you can get a drinking glass, a utensil, a napkin, anything we can run a DNA test on?"

"Do we have any DNA samples on Mansfield?"

"No, but at least we'd have something for future reference."

"I don't give a damn about future reference. I have a suspect in the hotel right now."

"Sir, there will be dire consequences if you cross that perimeter."

"I'll make sure you get your feckin' souvenirs. O'Shaughnessy out."

The MI6 agents were just as frustrated as O'Shaughnessy as the evening progressed. The militants carefully watched as the chinaware and silverware were carried in and out of the ballroom. Their enforcers in the hallways watched to see that no one entered the service areas to pick up samples. They knew that it was not possible to confirm that nothing was swiped by MI6, but at least no one would be in danger of being identified and tailed immediately after leaving the hotel. The agents, in turn, had been duly warned by their superiors that anyone caught gathering evidence at the event would be subject to severe disciplinary action. 'Caught' seemed to be the keyword, yet it remained a daunting task.

---

1. Facial Features Identification
2. Secret Intelligence Service

The event finally came to an end after a sumptuous dinner featuring Irish lamb shank with rosemary mashed potatoes. The champagne, wine and liquor continued to flow as the mass murderers and serial killers among the diplomats and politicians slowly made their way to the exits. Everyone was greatly impressed by the banquet and felt greatly at ease after having rubbed elbows with government agents and mortal enemies alike to no consequence. They were fairly sure that the guarantees would be kept as they prepared for the more serious discussions ahead.

Jennifer herself was feeling somewhat subdued though maintaining a jovial demeanor in wishing everyone a pleasant evening. She had suppressed her emotions and desires for years after her wedding to Prince Conrad, and felt almost like Elizabeth I in portraying a Virgin Queen without blemish for the past few years. Jim Jones had kindled a spark inside her she had not felt in a very long time. If she were in Scotland, she would have had someone invite him to her table. Here in Belfast, she had to watch Jones leave the ballroom as they passed each other like ships in the night. She was both melancholy and distracted as she left the Hastings Hotel with her chauffeur and bodyguard shortly after midnight.

The tires of her black Mercedes Benz squealed as it peeled away from the entrance of the hotel, seeking to avoid the paparazzi she knew would be on her trail. Jennifer was in the rear seat, with her chauffeur and her bodyguard in the front of the vehicle. The driver went against traffic on Great Victoria Street, making a sharp left in veering towards the dogleg on Brunswick Street. As the Mercedes made its turn, Jon Stevens and Slash Scimitar noticed that it was being tailed by a black motorcycle, a dark sedan and a white Fiat.

"Something's going on," Jon nudged Slash as they stood at a distance from the Crown Bar across the street from the hotel. "Let's go check it out."

The CIA agents sprinted down the street, turning the corner as the sedan began tail-gating the Mercedes. They were both in top shape and raced to the scene where the Mercedes was being forced to make a left on Bains Place. The Fiat gunned its motor as it overtook the Mercedes, nearly sideswiping it in forcing it to the right into the parking lot adjacent to the nearby Travelodge. The motorcycle then shot past the Mercedes into the deserted parking lot. The rider made a donut turn in front of the Mercedes, firing a laser beam into the windshield in blinding the driver. The chauffeur lost control as the Mercedes careened into a lamppost and flipped onto its side. The Fiat came to a halt thirty yards from the crash as the sedan did a U-turn and headed back up Brunswick.

"Sons of bitches," Jon huffed, beckoning Slash to follow him to the upended Mercedes. "That's got to be the Princess in there. That's her car."

Almost as if on cue, Jennifer managed to open one of the windows and climb shakily from the wreck. She saw the two agents rushing towards her and crouched as if to flee.

"Hold on!" Jon yelled. "We're Americans! We're here to help you!"

She started to run but stopped again as the two passengers in the Fiat emerged from the car and began running towards her. She could also see the black-leathered biker watching from the distance.

"It's okay," one of the men called over. "We're security, we'll handle it from here."

"Sure you will," Slash smirked. "They sent you to the ball dressed as bums."

"You hold them off," Jon rushed over to Jennifer, kicking a beer bottle across the pavement to Slash. It broke as he picked it up, waving it menacingly at the attackers as Jon grabbed Jennifer's arm.

"Look, there's a ton of security on Great Victoria. Let's cut through the bar and you'll be safe."

"I really don't think this is the time or place to stop for a pint," she managed.

They darted up an alley to the lot behind the Crown Bar, which was crowded with tourists, students and couples enjoying the unusually warm weather. More than a few customers were taken aback at the familiar face of the beautiful woman in formal wear being ushered through the pub by the grim-faced young man.

"Look, it's Princess Jennifer!" people began calling out.

"Those men are after me!" she pointed to her pursuers, who had taken Slash down and were shoving their way through the rear doorway. "Please help me!"

Jon continued steering Jennifer towards the Great Victoria entrance as a number of college kids in the crowd began blocking the path of the aggressors. He could see the door ahead of them and pushed ahead of her, grabbing her hand as he barged forth.

"Aye, and it's a sorry day in the Kingdom when criminals are chasing the Princess of Edinburgh through the streets," an older woman shook her head.

Jon plowed through the door, looking down the street as the security forces were deployed at the corner of Brunswick. He started moving in that direction when he found himself surrounded by four men on the sidewalk. He threw a groin kick at the closest man, dropping him with a straight right before being blindsided with a roundhouse punch that staggered him. Jon saw Jennifer being grabbed with his peripheral vision before he was tackled to the pavement.

"Tell them if they don't end the peace talks, the bitch dies," a man snarled at him.

"Why don't you tell them yourself, dick breath, they're right up the corner," Jon shot back before they took him out with a boot to the jaw.

* * *

It was early Saturday morning when the three Glider Jeeps rolled up Shankill Road and parked in front of the King William Social Club. There were ten men in all, a four-man fire team in camouflage fatigues carrying rifles in the front and rear vehicles. The middle vehicle carried a rifleman along with a khaki-clad commando wearing a SAS beret. The four Ulster Freedom Fighters dressed in black in front of the club were quick to announce the presence of Mark O'Shaughnessy to those inside.

"Mark, it's great to see you," Ed Doherty stood at a card table towards the back of the small but cozy lounge. The mahogany bar was off to his far left, a pinball machine alongside the doorframe. There was a space off to his right where two other tables and chairs sat empty at this time of day. The bartender glanced up at the newcomer and made himself busy in the back room adjoining the bar. Two more gunmen wearing dark blazers sat at the bar while Delmore Merrick sat at the table alongside Doherty.

"Little early for that, Del?" Mark nodded at the glass of Bushmill's on the table before the thin, white-haired, red-nosed man.

"That'd depend on what time your day starts," Merrick stared evenly at him.

"Coffee," Doherty barked at the bartender. "Coffee for our guest here."

"How's business?" Mark sat down on the chair facing the two gang leaders, the wooden chair straining under his 6'4", 300-pound bulk. He looked at his coffee cup with the UFF logo emblazoned over the Red Hand of Ulster. "Selling lots of these things, are you?"

"Not bad, not bad," Doherty allowed. "Lots of patriots out there these days, the world being in the state it's in."

"You've been here a long time," Mark glanced around. "What's it now, going on forty years? I've seen lots of bosses come and go, but you've survived and prospered. You've always known how to ride the tide, keep your head above water through good times and bad."

"Aye, I suppose it's all about making sure everything's in order at the end of your shift. Always making sure everything remains safe and sound on your watch. That's all your people ask, when all's said and done."

"All was not in order on my watch last night. I'm sure someone hereabouts switched on the telly and saw all the rumpus about that girl getting snatched yesterday."

"Surely it'll all be sorted out in due time. All they have to do is look around. Ulster's not that big a place. She's got to be somewhere. Why, there, in fact. There she is. Come here, my Princess. There she is, good girl!"

Mark managed a chuckle and shook his head as a small black kitten bounded up onto Doherty's lap.

"Her name's not Princess, it's Shirley," Merrick grunted.

"There, you see?" Doherty waved towards him. "Always a wiseguy."

"I've got eight riflemen sitting in jeeps outside who are ready and willing to tear this block up to look for her. Now, of course I know they wouldn't find anything, but the next fellow who comes out here might not be so certain."

"Come now, Mark, surely you realize you're on the wrong side of town. This is the East Side, you need to be over on the West Side where those militants reside. You know the people on this side are peaceful folk. We wave the Union Jack proudly throughout our community. Patriots we are, and patriots we'll always be. What on earth would make you think we'd have anything to do with snatching a Princess of the Realm?"

"I don't know," Mark sipped his coffee, raising his eyebrows at the robust flavor. "Lots of old-timers hereabouts may not be too happy about the lass' agenda, making peace with the Republicans. There's always going to be those delusions about Ulster seceding from the UK and uniting with the South. Of course, you and I know better. We know it's more about all these Unionist militias having to disband and lose a whole lot of money in the process."

"There, you said it," Doherty cocked his head. "Delusions and rumors. Parliament has suggested that these so-called paramilitary organizations are worth millions of pounds. Look around you, fellow. Look at Delmore and myself. Do you see anything that looks like a million pounds anywhere around here?"

"All I ask is that you keep an ear to the ground, and let me know immediately if you see or hear anything. It's not just us, you know. My boss got a call from the Prime Minister this morning. He got a call from the President of the United States. This has turned into very serious business on my end. Certainly you realize that if it's serious business on my end, it's bound to seriously hurt your business."

"I'm just a poor man trying to make ends meet, Mark," Doherty raised his hands innocently. "You overestimate me, my old friend. I stand behind some thrones here and there, I whisper in some ears, but wise folks are always ready to listen to those of age and experience. Rest assured if any of our people suspect where those IRA kidnappers may be holding our beloved Princess, we'll notify you immediately."

"Please do. You might pause to consider that in the course of this crackdown on insurgent activity, MI6 will be a lot more likely to interfere in criminal enterprise they might not ordinarily involve themselves in. We've been hearing rumors about a shipment of narcotics from London to Belfast that's been having trouble finding safe harbor. Now, of course, if the girl was returned safe and sound as a result of your cooperation, I could see where a certain activity or its consequence might be overlooked. On the other hand, this crisis situation could very well create countless inconveniences to all concerned."

"Mark," Doherty looked pained. "After all these years, how could you speak to me this way? You know my edict concerning drugs. In my neighborhood, you deal you die! Not that I could directly influence such a thing, but I would never raise a hand to prevent the demise of any slimeball who would bring this social disease into our communities, among our women and children."

"Of course," O'Shaughnessy finished his coffee, rising to leave. "Say, do you think you could have a box of these cups shipped over to the base? They'd be jolly good conversation pieces, souvenirs to take back home."

"My pleasure. How about some T-shirts?"

"That'd be a bit over the top. Gentlemen, a pleasure as always. Be sure and call as soon as you hear anything."

The occupants of the club waited until they heard the jeeps drive away.

"Those stupid bastards!" Doherty choked, causing the kitten to race away. "Has everyone lost their feckin' minds? Did you give them the order to snatch that bitch?"

"Edward, the man stood on the carpet in front of you and the fellas from London the other night, asking your permission," Merrick said evenly. "The man even placed a report on your table explaining how he was going to do it. You threw it in the trash, and now you're wondering as to what came of it."

"I don't give a shit about any of that! Reason with me, Del! Leaving a piece of paper on my table does not give a man permission to kidnap the Princess of the feckin' UK!"

"There's a stack of reports in your desk drawer," Merrick exhaled. "Debating the issue won't make it go away. They've got the woman in a safe house and have called for instructions as to what to do next."

"We're up to our necks now, Ed," one of his top enforcers, Skull Murphy, sat at the bar. "We can't just let her go. We've got to be able to place blame without taking responsibility. Yet we can't leave those kids hanging to dry. I say we call a War Council meeting to see how the leadership wants to handle this."

"Are ye blootered, Murphy? I'm going to stand on the carpet and admit I let those young jackasses kidnap the Princess without my permission?"

"You gave permission," Merrick sipped his whiskey.

"Shut up, Delmore," Doherty snapped. "Look, just tell them to keep her on ice until we can sort it all out. In the meantime, we still have to take possession of that shipment coming in from London. This is Cody's responsibility, that crazy son of a bitch. He's my top smuggler. How is he going to be in two places at once? You need to tell him he needs to get on top of this situation with my delivery as soon as possible. Even O'Shaughnessy knows about it, for god's sakes. Have him lock her away and get on the ball with my delivery, got it?"

"That'll be fine. Have you decided what to do about the supergrass up in Omagh?"

"Aye, I'm sending Red October. At least we know that'll be a job done right."

"Red October?" Merrick squinted as the others stared at Doherty. "Are you sure you want to go that far?"

"Things are slipping, they're getting out of hand," Doherty said quietly. "It's time to let people know we're no longer feckin' around. No more Mr. Nice Guy."

* * *

Jon Stevens and Slash Scimitar found themselves back at Fritz Hammer's hotel room on Great Eastern Street later that day. They had been brought in for questioning and produced their 'Get Out Of Jail' cards that the CIA gave their field operatives. Soon they were transported to an MI6 command center outside Belfast where they were debriefed. Afterwards they were driven to Madison's Hotel on Botanic Avenue, within walking distance of Queen's University. They called Fritz that morning and took a cab to the Hoxton Hotel a few hours later.

"You fellows have certainly returned to the spotlight," Fritz informed him as they sat in his room once again. They brought a four-pack of Guinness and he popped a top along with them. They had a strong reputation as street operatives and were far more productive when reporting to a superior who was 'one of the guys'. "You were the last ones to have seen the Princess. Both the President and the Prime Minister were very interested in what you had to say."

"Very good looking woman," Jon replied. "Responded well under pressure."

"Since you're knee-deep in this already, we intend to keep you on the field to see this through. I wanted to get suggestions as to how you would want to proceed."

"I was hoping to mix business with pleasure."

"That is not making me feel very confident. I recall some unpleasant rumors in Kosovo a few years ago. It seems there were questions about some ill-gotten gains and windfall profits you both enjoyed during a sting operation against some Albanian militants."

"C'mon, Fritz," Jon objected mildly. "We set the whole thing up with intelligence officers with the Serbian Army, and we were working closely with the Kosovo Police. We practically put the entire brigade out of business and put some bad guys behind bars. I think we should've gotten a commendation for that one."

"A half ton of heroin disappeared into thin air after the investigation. Less than a couple of years later, you purchased a four million dollar mansion on Long Island and Slash buys one of his own in Grenada. It is understandable that a few eyebrows were raised."

"Hey, you do what you can in this economy. Everybody's looking for that parachute when they retire. There were some decent investment opportunities in Europe that we didn't overlook, put it that way."

"What is it you have in mind here?" Fritz came to the point.

"Nothing extravagant. I was thinking about a bike shop somewhere like Lower Ormeau Road, on a borderline area between the Catholic and Protestant neighborhoods. If the Company can underwrite a loan, I have a cousin who lives in the Republic. I think I can get him to come up here and run the place for me."

"A bike shop? As in motorcycles?"

"Motorcycles are big here in Ireland. This is one of the most popular riding spots in Europe. It's not unusual to see bikers in all areas of the country, which is what makes it such a good cover. People aren't going to think of it as unusual to see bikers out in the middle of nowhere looking for directions. If we can get some of the biker clubs to cooperate with us, it'd be like a clandestine search force. It'd also give us an idea whose side the clubs are on. If there's a couple of gangs who give us a hard time, it'll be easier to see which ones are lined up with the militants on either side."

"It's not the worst idea I've heard today," Fritz admitted. "Just so long as you realize it's a loan, not a matching investment for your retirement program."

"Hey, I'll get the cheapest spot I can find. This business pays for any remodeling or improvements we need beyond getting the doors open. I'll put together a grand opening celebration, have a band, send out invitations and go from there."

"You'll be in direct contact with Colonel Mark O'Shaughnessy with the SAS. He's my mirror as MI6's military liaison. We'll give you a phone number to London and they'll set it up from there. There's so much collusion going on here, you'll have no direct contacts with the police or the paramilitary. We have no idea who's behind the kidnapping, so you'll regard both the Republicans and the Unionist activists as hostiles. In other words, the only friends you have out here is the ones you make on your own. O'Shaughnessy's your go-to guy. If there's any problems you contact Division Headquarters directly."

"Sounds like fun. When can I start writing checks?"

"We'll give you the name of the bank by tomorrow. We'll start you off with twenty grand, if you need more there'll be a contact number."

"Great. Hopefully we'll have the Princess back by the end of the week."

* * *

That evening, Berlin Mansfield had five of his closest and most trusted associates flown out to Belfast International Airport and transported to the Hotel Europa, which had recovered sufficiently from the kidnapping to resume business as usual. They next converged at Deane's Restaurant on Howard Street where they were afforded one of the establishment's signature dinners, including entrees of Lough Erne beef and Fermenagh chicken. The group was in a jovial mood, regaling each other with anecdotes about their recent personal exploits. They were cautious never to discuss any of their previous joint projects, and were not sure why Mansfield had brought them to Belfast this weekend.

"So you heard about that thing that went down last night at that hotel we're staying at? Typical Berlin," Kurt the Bruiser chuckled. His International Wrestling Association was one of the hottest promotions on the globe, incorporating shoot wrestling fights with their pro wrestling performance bouts. "The cops probably squeezed that place out so hard last night, it'd be the last place to look for guys like us."

"Actually I was there, before the snatch, of course," Mansfield smiled, pouring himself a glass of champagne from one of the iced bottles. If I would've known what was going to happen, I would've offered her a ride."

"So what were you doing there, testing your new disguise?" Benny Van Tran chuckled. He ran one of the biggest private security services in Iraq for corporate enterprises from around the world. They had not recognized Mansfield in the lobby until he walked up to them.

"I was there visiting an old friend, who just happened to be with the IRA delegates. The dinner was quite excellent, almost as good as this."

"Yeah, that's because you paid for this one," Al 'the Cat' Catano snickered. He was a fiber optics engineer who was considered one of the world's top surveillance experts.

"So what was the big rush with this?" Sting Ramapril held his hands out, leaning back in his chair. He was the leader of one of the biggest smuggling gangs in the Caribbean. Each of the men had financed their operations with the money they had earned with Mansfield over the years, and remained loyal to him. "I had some pretty hot dates lined up. I had to cancel one to make that flight."

"You should talk. I was supposed to be in Chechnya tomorrow night," Chuck 'Chopper' Valentine grunted. He was one of the world's most notorious human organ traffickers for the international Chinese networks. "Don't get any ideas of calling on New Year's Eve, pal, because the best you're gonna get is an obscene recording."

"I know I'm calling in my markers tonight," Mansfield dipped a slice of potato in Béarnaise sauce. "Sometimes things come up in life, and you just never know who to call. The first thing you think of is friends, but you never really know who they are in this business. The only way to find out is when you see who shows up."

"Okay, so hail, hail, the gang's all here," Chuck Chop leaned back in his chair, folding his hands in his lap. "So now maybe you can explain to me why I'm in Belfast instead of Grozny tonight."

"First a toast. To old friends, and my deepest appreciation for all of you being here," Mansfield insisted. They filled their glasses with champagne and waited until he raised his, the gang toasting one another before taking a sip.

"So what's going on, do you have cancer?" Chuck asked before a chorus of laughter.

"It's a matter of honor on my part. Technically I was part of the security force last night. She was taken on my watch. I feel as if it would be an insult to me if word got out."

"Are you kidding? She's probably dead by now," Kurt scoffed. "That was like snatching the President. They'll never stop looking for the perps, and when they find them they'll put 'em away for the rest of their lives. They gotta take her out so they can't be identified."

"They must want something," Mansfield decided. "A ransom, perhaps. Or maybe they'll hold her until the talks are indefinitely suspended, as they demanded. If the team remains unidentified, no one will know if the IRA or the UDA is responsible. Therefore neither side could be trusted if another negotiation was proposed."

"All right, drum roll, the million-dollar question," Al grinned. "Who's paying and how much?"

"No one," Mansfield looked around the table. "Nothing."

There was a long pause.

"Let me wrap my head around this," Kurt leaned forward. "You want us to help you rescue the Princess, *pro bono*. This is in the middle of a nationwide manhunt led by the most efficient Special Forces unit on the planet, who would put any one of us in jail for the rest of our lives if we're caught with Berlin Mansfield."

"You know what they say," Mansfield smiled softly. "It never hurts to ask."

"Okay, guys," Chuck Chop tossed his napkin on the round banquet table, "Berlin's just pulling our puds here. "Everyone knows that Civil War II in Africa's gonna be one of the biggest and bloodiest battles of all time. He's already got a deal in the works, and if we don't take the bait on this we get crossed off the list for the next one. I don't know about you guys, but if I take the next one I expect to walk away with enough so I never have to go out again. I'd even plan on closing down my body bag business."

"Actually I don't have any offers on the next one, Chopper. Not yet."

"Yeah, sure, whatever. Go ahead, count me in."

"You've already saved my life more times than I can remember," Kurt poured another glass of champagne. "Of course, it goes without saying that my life wouldn't have been in danger if I hadn't gotten involved in any of your capers. What the hell, I'm in, you only live once, right?"

"I've got a wife and kids," Sting spoke up. "So does Al and Benny. My family's the most important thing in the world to me. I know if anything ever happened and my family was in danger, there is one guy in the world I can call and I could bet my life he'd be there. For that reason alone I'll go along with this."

"Shit," Al scowled. "Now we're gonna play the sympathy card. What'd you two do, rehearse this? Go ahead, put me down, all I got to lose is time and money."

"So everyone's actually going along with this?" Benny stared around in disbelief. "Rescuing the Princess of Edinburgh for no money whatsoever."

"You'd be the odd man out, but I can't say you wouldn't be missed," Mansfield also noted the looks of resignation on the faces at the table.

"You gonna at least cover our room and board?" Benny asked plaintively.

"It would be my pleasure."

* * *

Jennifer Mac Manus had been in captivity for over twenty-four hours, and it had been the most grueling ordeal of her life.

She had been thrown into the trunk of the dark sedan when she was grabbed off the sidewalk in front of the Crown Bar. After a couple of miles of zigzagging the car stopped long enough for her to be bound and gagged. She was doing her best to remain calm and rational but she was frightened out of her wits. She had done enough research to know that most of the militants in the struggle gave not one whit about human life. It was not beyond reason to think she might be driven to a garage, stood up before a video camera and shot in the middle of a political harangue.

They brought her to a barn where she was blindfolded and carried inside. She was fastened to a post by the wrist with a four-foot chain which allowed her to put on a pair of sweat pants, socks and sneakers beneath her evening gown. They then switched the chain to her ankle so she could pull off the gown in exchange for a T-shirt and a sweatshirt. She begged and pleaded but they told her to shut up, giving her a roll of soda bread and a container of milk. After she ate they bound and gagged her again, throwing her back in the car trunk before taking off once more.

Eventually they ended up at a farmhouse some time before dawn, and she was again blindfolded and led into the house up a flight of stairs. She was tossed onto a bed and she could feel her left ankle chained to a post before she was completely untied. She rubbed her eyes and saw a lone figure sitting on a chair by the bed in the dark room.

"Who are you? What do you want?"

"You can call me Cody. I'm with the Protestant Liberation Organization."

"The PLO? Come on, I know who the PLO is."

"Does it really matter at this point?"

"Are you—going to kill me?"

"I doubt it."

"You doubt it?" Jennifer broke a cold sweat. "Did you contact anyone? I'm sure they'd offer money for you to let me go."

"What makes you so sure we'd take it?"

"Then why are you doing this?" she insisted.

"That's the trouble with your kind," the man was dressed in a black workout suit and combat boots, wearing a ski mask. "You think it's all about money. We don't give a damn about money. We're here to make sure Ulster remains part of the United Kingdom. You've no call to sell our birthright for a bowl of Irish stew."

"Selling you out?" Jennifer could not help herself. "No one's selling you out. Look how well the people down South are doing, much less my own brothers and sisters in Scotland. Don't you think we could do better here? If you people would just quit fighting amongst yourselves we could accomplish so much together."

"I'm a soldier, I'm not a politician," Cody rose to leave. "I don't know enough about those things to argue with you. All I'm telling you is that I've got a man in a hallway who will bind and gag you and have you thrown back in a car trunk if you make noise. There's a pot and paper under the bed if you've got to potty. I've got someone out running errands. For your information, none of us have eaten since we grabbed you, so you'll have to bear with us. When he gets back we'll breakfast, and then we'll move on to somewhere else."

"Have you contacted the police? Have you sent word to anyone?"

"I've contacted my superiors and I'm waiting for word from them. Don't expect to get released anytime soon, there are a lot of issues to be resolved here. We wouldn't have done this if your Government had not bent over backwards to deal with these terrorists. There are a number of concessions that will have to be agreed to, and they won't be accepted from the Chief of Police. There are going to be a lot of people looking for you, so we're going to be on the move. It'll be a whole lot easier on you if you cooperate. I'm here to tell you that if you and I can trust each other, we can help one another get through this. Agreed?"

"I'm really hungry and thirsty," she pleaded. "Can I at least have a glass of water?"

"There's a bottle of water and a packet of crackers under there as well. I'll just have you know those were my crackers."

"Thank you."

"Don't forget, no noise," he walked out and locked the door behind him.

She pulled out the bedpan and took a blessed leak, then devoured the crackers and took her time savoring the water before pulling the covers up from the foot of the bed. She shivered with comfort as she pulled them up around her, fighting off her fear as she plummeted into an exhausted, dreamless sleep.

Chapter Three

Deryl Lee Kilmarnoch was a traveling man. He was born in Nashville and fell in love with the music scene along the downtown area. He was even more intrigued by the wild and wooly bikers who cruised along Broadway on week-ends, their tattoos proudly proclaiming they were 'Born to Raise Hell.' He was a charismatic type, big for his age, a friendly auburn-haired, green-eyed kid with the gift of blarney. He built his first dirt bike when he was a teenager, and became the mascot of the Iron Claw Motorcycle Club until they helped him get his own Harley-Davidson. From that day on he became a biker and never looked back.

He and his cousin Jon Stevens were the mavericks of the family, and everyone thought it was an act of God that resulted in both men being sent to Grenada as part of the American invasion in 1984. Jon was with Delta Force and Deryl Lee was with the Navy SEALs. They partied hardy after the sweep of Communist revolutionaries by the USA forces and promised to keep in touch. Only Jon signed up with the CIA shortly thereafter, and Deryl Lee set out on a motorcycle odyssey across Europe. The cousins saw each other a couple of times during the Serbian War, but Deryl Lee grew tired of the strife on the Continent and bought a home in Sligo, Ireland.

He got a call from Jon and agreed to meet him in Belfast to discuss a business proposal. He was glad to hear from him again and packed a bag to take the long bike ride across the border of Ulster. He enjoyed living along the countryside and considered trips into town as events. Meeting with his cousin in the capitol city would certainly be a time to remember. He also knew there were a lot of great pubs in the area that he would visit on the way back.

Jon and Slash arrived at 10 AM at Bittles Bar, one of the landmark establishments in downtown Belfast. Deryl was already digging into a plate of Ulster fry, but was not overly surprised to see the partners order pints of Guinness before coming over to join him.

"You fellows start early, don't you?" Deryl grinned, wiping his hands as he got up to meet them.

"Depends what you call early," Slash replied as they put down their glasses, the cousins hugging and pounding one another's backs. Deryl and Slash next shook hands before they took seats at the wooden table in the traditional pub-style establishment.

"We're planning to open up a bike shop along Lower Ormeau Road not far from here," Jon explained after they exchanged pleasantries and anecdotes. "It's kinda along the DMZ between the Caddy and Proddy neighborhoods. Obviously we're not gonna be around all year to keep the place running, so we were wondering if you'd like to manage the place. We were figuring on a big opening, give us a chance to build up a contact list. We'll be in town for a few weeks, we can get it up and running, give you a chance to hire an assistant manager. That'd give you a chance to get your own priorities in order between here and Sligo. There's no rush or anything. You take whatever you make, pay the bills, send us a cut and keep the rest."

"Sounds great to me. When were you planning to get started?"

"We can drive over and take a look at the place now. If it works for you, I'll call the remodelers and the bike dealerships. We'll get in touch with some print shops, caterers, and plan on a big-ass party in a week from now."

"You move fast, don'tcha, Cous?" Deryl grinned.

"You remember a time when I didn't?"

They drove to the partially-vacant block where the realtor awaited. There was a supermarket for lease alongside a storefront, and Jon quickly opted for the supermarket as the realtor gladly produced the paperwork.

"How much for the storefront?" Deryl asked. "I think I'd be able to find use for it."

"You'd probably be better off finding an apartment," Jon suggested.

"Oh, I will. I just thought I might want some extra space once we're up and running, which I suspect we'll be in a short time."

"That's the spirit, The Protestant work ethic."

The realtor gave Jon a funny look.

"We're Yanks," Jon explained. "It's just an American saying. No offense."

They signed the paperwork and headed back to Bittles Bar for drinks to celebrate the new partnership. Jon gave him their address at the Tara Lodge on Cromwell Road, as Deryl decided he would be looking for a bed and breakfast near the Queen's University where he could get situated and began setting up shop. He understood that the partners were in town on CIA business as they admitted the motorcycle dealership was going to be a front for their own operation. They further guaranteed that they would not be running any other business out of the shop, so he would not have to worry about any police involvement. Deryl said that would suit him just fine.

He decided to take lodging at Evelyn's Bed and Breakfast on Wellington Park Terrace, enjoying the camaraderie of the University students as he planned his next move. He had thought long and hard about relocating up north and getting involved in the struggle for peace. Only the way never seemed clear, and there was never a way to go about it without antagonizing one group or another. Now an idea was formulating in his head, and his cousin Jon seemed to be providing the opportunity to make something happen at last.

Deryl was somewhat amazed at how fast Jon put everything together. The remodelers were on site the next day, gutting the walls and installing fiberglass insulation, sheetrocking, taping and floating before painting. He next contacted a Harley Davidson dealership in London as well as the corporate offices of Titan Motorcycles in Phoenix, Arizona. They swiftly made a deal which was brokered by Universal Exports, the CIA's super-powered corporate front. They had a shipment of Fat Boy Harleys and Titan motorbikes guaranteed to ship on consignment within forty-eight hours.

After that, Jon took out a full page ad in the *Belfast Telegraph* announcing the grand opening next Saturday. He also took out a space in the *Queen's News*, the University newspaper, inviting the students as well as street performers and artists to come out and join in the festivities. He hired a local band, the Boys of Wexford, and ordered a couple of kegs of Guinness and Harp. They also planned to give out hot dogs and hamburgers, assuring that the affair would turn into a block party celebration.

Deryl's progress was somewhat less strident. He rented out a room in a nearby apartment building and had a handyman come by to refurbish the storefront. He rode back out to Sligo and packed a couple of bags, switching his Harley out for his Volvo and driving back for an extended stay. He still was unsure about how he would get his vision quest started from the storefront, but would wait until after the grand opening of American Choppers to decide.

Just as Jon figured, the event was as over-the-top as anything the neighborhood had seen in a long time. Word of mouth spread like wildfire as youngsters were recruited as volunteers to pass out flyers and help with the barbecue. He had hired a clown to give out balloons, and soon there was a procession of mothers and babysitters arriving with children to decorate the pavement with street chalk. The band set up and began playing, drawing crowds from the nearby campus and student hangouts. Every adult that came in to check out the bikes and sign the mailing list was able to sample a small cup of beer. It was not long before the police came out to monitor the event and assure that everything remained peaceful.

Deryl recognized a couple of the bikers who showed up from a couple of the circuit runs he had participated in when he first arrived in Sligo. He was introduced to other bikers who began arriving, which was what Jon was planning on. He came over and introduced himself, and it was not long before he was rubbing elbows with some of the leaders of biker gangs around Antrim County. He brought them to the back office individually where he was able to give them samples of some of the purple Hawaiian weed he had stashed away.

"Don't light this up around here, there's cops all over the place," he told each of them. "Just give me a call if you're interested in scoring some weight. We're almost out, but I can get you a great one-time deal. All I'm asking is that you put out the word that we're trying to get some information on the Princess kidnapping. I need to know if any of your guys see anything out on the road that looks suspicious. You know, some abandoned place that suddenly has people inside, or some out-of-the-way dirt road that suddenly has fresh tracks."

"This is some kind of American set-up, isn't it?" one of the bikers smirked. "You're not working with the Brits, are you?"

"Nope," Jon admitted, leaning back in the swivel chair behind the desk in the small office, facing Rory Calhoun of the Antrim Angel Dusters. "Let's just say there are private interests wanting to see the Princess come back in one piece. This isn't about politics, we're not trying to pin the tail on the donkey. We don't care who's got her, we just want her back, no questions asked."

"Well, I'll tell you, the Brits have got huge areas of the countryside locked down tight. They've got armored patrols, helicopters, checkpoints, every damned thing going on. Most of the clubs are heading south until this thing clears up. We're not the kind that cuts and runs, though, never have been and never will be. We'll still be riding the roads here in Antrim, so if we come across anything I'll let you know. What kind of prices are you talking, anyway?"

Jon scribbled some figures on the back of a business card and pushed it across the desk.

"The top price is the going rate. The second price is yours if you get me some info."

"You got a deal, mate. I'll put out the word with the other clubs. Lots of people owe me favors here in Ulster."

It was Monday morning by the time Deryl had an idea of what he wanted to do. He showed up at his storefront at 7 AM with a placard and a thick marker, and created a sign in thick block letters which he pinned on the front door: A PLACE TO PRAY.

He went next door and took a dozen of the folding chairs that they had used for the grand opening, setting them up in his storefront. He then went to his knees and prayed to the Lord for guidance. He decided this would be his new routine from 7:30 to 8:30 each morning before he opened American Choppers at 9 AM. It would not conflict with his duties as manager, and would give him the quality time he needed to put his plan into action.

On the third day a couple of the elderly women in the neighborhood began coming in and sitting down to pray. Some carried rosaries while others brought their Bibles. Deryl had brought his PC with him, and printed a Prayer for Peace which he set out on a table by the door. Before he locked up on Friday, he stood at the makeshift podium he erected at the front of the store. He said the prayer along with the Our Father, and the women joined in unison.

"I'd like you all to spread the word that all are invited to join us next week," he announced before they left the store. "We'll be here to pray for the peace of Northern Ireland. Our people have suffered long enough. People of all religions are welcome, this isn't about politics. This is a place where we can all get together as neighbors and believers in Christ. This is a place where we can pray for miracles to happen."

He wasn't entirely sure of why he was doing this, but he knew that the people of Ireland had surely had enough. His Daddy had been a preacher as had his granddaddy before him. He never had the calling and was unsure whether he had it now. What he did know is that he had wanted to get involved for a long time, and this seemed to be as good a time as ever. He would let the Holy Ghost guide his steps, and let the chips fall where they may.

He never dreamed that he would be drawn into the vortex as quickly or as drastically as he was in a very short time ahead.

* * *

Shannon Blackburn was a country girl who lived with her family near the fishing village of Dundalk along the border of the Republic. She was six years old when her parents were murdered by UDA volunteers in a politically-motivated assassination. Extremist groups in the area had sent death threats to families in the area suspected of supporting Republican militants around Dundalk. The Blackburns were put on a list despite the fact they were guilty of nothing but having been baptized Catholic as infants.

After the murder, two of her father's second cousins stepped up and claimed Shannon, assuring the surviving family that they would provide for her. It was well-known that they had converted to the Protestant faith for material gain, and were prospering so that the family thought it would be a good thing for the orphaned girl. They took her to their farm property along the outskirts of town, and that was where her nightmare began.

She was immediately put to work as a servant, carrying out all the chores around the rundown property under threat of being severely beaten. The two brothers were degenerate alcoholics, and made their living selling drugs and homemade liquor. She had only one change of clothing and was allowed to bathe with hot water only once a week. She lived on soups and leftovers, and was terrorized by the fighting dogs they kept on the property, who they would set on her if she dared try and escape.

They celebrated her thirteenth birthday by taking her virginity, and sexual abuse became part of her daily ordeal. She endured the tortures of the damned for three more years, until one day the brothers learned that they were being hunted by the RUC[1] and would have to abandon the farm indefinitely. The older brother set out to find them a safe house along the border, instructing his sibling to prepare to relocate along with Shannon upon his return.

By now, Shannon was just as familiar with the house and the surrounding property as the brothers. She also knew their habits and routines, and was fi-

---

1. Royal Ulster Constabulary

nally in position to carry out a plan she had formulated over the years. She had been dusting the dregs of their narcotics into a tiny beaker when she cleaned up after their partying. It was finally enough for a time like this. She waited until the older brother departed, then brought out a syringe she had swiped and prepared a solution. The younger brother got drunk and passed out, forgetting to lock Shannon in the cellar after dinner as was their routine.

Shannon snuck up on the dozing man and injected the solution into his jugular vein. He started after her but she managed to elude his clutches until he collapsed. She managed to drag him into the bathroom, then bound and gagged him in the bathtub. She then brought in a bucket of dog food and began cutting off strips of his flesh, bringing portions out to feed to the dogs. It took two days before he finally bled to death.

Her uncle told her everything she needed to know about the house before he died. She was able to call her other uncle and tell him that there had been an accident. His brother had been injured and he was needed back home immediately. He arrived at the house a few hours later, and when he walked through the door Shannon gut-shot him with a small-caliber pistol. She dragged him to the bathroom, where he managed to survive one day longer than his brother had under the same treatment.

By now the Dundalk UDA was in a quandary. Their connections were pressing hard for the whereabouts of the Blackburns, and the order was given by the UDA leadership to murder the wayward brothers. A hit squad arrived at the farm under cover of darkness, and even the hardcore killers were astounded by what they found. The fighting dogs had been feeding exclusively from the dismembered bodies of their dead masters. They inspected Shannon and were appalled by the terrible abuse the girl had suffered. They brought her back to their headquarters where an emergency meeting was called to decide what to do next.

Eddie Doherty happened to be in Dundalk on business, and he offered to bring the girl back to Belfast with him. The callous racketeer was disturbed by her situation and thought he might be able to find a place where she could be of use. He set her up with a UDA widow who was also touched by Shannon's plight. After she was cleaned up and properly fed, they marveled at how beautiful the auburn-haired, blue-eyed girl was. They only hoped that she would lose her vacant, soulless gaze in time.

The dowager was a retired schoolteacher, and she was greatly pleased to find how intelligent Shannon was. She quickly brought Shannon up to speed in a number of subjects though the girl had not attended school in nearly a decade. She found that Shannon had an artistic spirit and greatly enjoyed poetry and classical music. Only she noticed that the girl had a violent reaction to disturbances, and did her best to make sure the cottage was calm as possible at all times.

Doherty came by on a regular basis to check on Shannon, and offered to take her on a ride to the countryside one Sunday afternoon after church. The girl was glad to accompany Uncle Eddie, and they drove out to the seashore where they had a long talk. Eddie told her about her uncles, the kind of men they were and the trouble they got themselves into. He used this to segue into telling her the history of the UDA and its struggle to defend the people of Ulster from forcible secession from the United Kingdom. He explained how her uncles had disgraced the organization and forsaken the sacred mission to which they had been entrusted.

"I want to give you the chance to redeem the honor of your family," Doherty explained. "There are other men who have done the kind of things your uncles have done. I want to know if you would be willing to bring justice to these men. The law in this area is useless and weak. They expect the UDA to carry out their duties for them. Only we've lost lots of good men in this struggle. I knew that you were someone special in being able to escape the terrible situation you were in. I know you have the strength to do the things that the people of Ulster require."

He told her he would be willing to pay her £25,000 for the assignment. It would be enough to cover a year's rent in her own apartment with plenty left over to cover her personal expenses. His lieutenants would give her detailed instructions, all the equipment and material she would need, and cover any expenses she incurred. When she was told it was a supergrass[2] who had a history of rape and sexual abuse charges, she readily agreed.

The murder was intended to be carried out as a warning to other squealers within the organization. The target was under police surveillance and was moving about West Belfast with impunity, certain that the UDA would not make a move against him in Catholic territory. Shannon waited for her victim to leave

---

2. police informer

a local nightclub after closing before walking up and shooting the detectives who were watching over him in their parked vehicle. She then shot him with a taser gun and stuffed him in a car trunk, injecting him with morphine before driving him to a secluded cottage outside city limits.

A week later, his dismembered body was found in a dumpster, having died in the same fashion as her uncles. Police determined that his eyes, ears, nose, lips, fingers and toes had all been removed while he was alive. The removal of his penis and testicles caused him to die of shock. They estimated he had endured the ordeal for three days before dying of his wounds. An intense manhunt was initiated for the killer but the police had no clues to work with and the investigation was soon curtailed.

They sent her out three months later, and she was able to buy her own home with her earnings. She was invited to a Christmas dinner reserved for high-ranking UDA officials, and rumor had spread as to who she was and what she had done. One particularly belligerent battalion leader got drunk and began belittling her as the only woman attending the elite gathering. The man disappeared a couple of days later. It was only after his body parts were found around town that the leadership began to suspect what happened. Eddie Doherty was called on the carpet and Shannon was exonerated shortly thereafter.

She was only called upon for the most important assignments after that, and was given the code name Red October. Her name had become synonymous with the death sentence, and rumors circulated that she had sold her soul to the Devil. Most of those who met her in person agreed that she seemed to display sociopathic tendencies, as if her mind and thoughts were a thousand miles away. Eddie Doherty was the only person she communicated with, and he visited her regularly to nurture their relationship.

It was the evening of the grand opening event of American Choppers that provided the UDA with a diversion allowing Red October to strike again. A supergrass was being kept under watch at the Merchant Hotel on Skipper Street. It was determined he had a room on the second floor of the stately hotel with an armed guard outside his door. She was paid her normal wage but warned that this would be an extremely perilous assignment.

The plainclothes detective outside the informant's door was caught offguard by the beautiful hooker who came up the stairs shortly after dark. She gave him the name of one of his colleagues who she said sent her to keep him company. He was about to run her off but her knockout body in her skimpy purple dress made it impossible for him to dismiss her so abruptly. She fondled him expertly, going down on her knees to continue her foreplay. His worst nightmare was realized as she had a razor device concealed in her mouth. He collapsed into shock as she took his gun, badge and room key before barging in on her next victim.

The informer stared in shock as the woman barged in, blood running from her mouth as a vampire. She used her taser gun to drop him to the carpet, producing a switchblade and cutting his pants from the crotch. She then cut off his penis and testicles, quickly replacing them with a feminine napkin.

"Now then," she smiled. "I'll trade these back if you give me the name of your undercover connection. They can find your body with your parts in place, or the papers can report to all of Belfast that you were found with a tampon in your bloody hole."

The man knew he was dying and he wanted to go out with dignity. He gave her the name she wanted, and she obligingly gave him his organs back in exchange for the tampon.

"Isn't it odd?" she said, hearing a commotion outside as someone had discovered the body in the hallway. "A couple of men die of blood loss and the entire city heads the ball. A woman loses a pint of blood a day and society hands her one of these."

She tossed the tampon in a waste basket and closed the door softly behind her.

Chapter Four

Jennifer Mac Manus woke up that Sunday morning, a few hours after Antrim County had been stunned by the double homicide at the Merchant Hotel. She was puffing on her Yachtsman cigarette, preparing herself for the task at hand. She had been held captive for nine days, and though there was a nationwide search in progress she had not seen a sign of rescuers in the vicinity. She was being held in a farmhouse in Portmuck outside Larne, and her abductors left only to pick up supplies or exchange messages in town. They would not even use their cell phones out here in fear of being traced.

The ennui had resulted in them lightening up on her. Baxter Cody brought her newspapers and magazines, though she noticed they had cut out articles on the kidnapping which often resulted in the first five pages being snipped out. Her meals were brought up by Cave Cat Sammy, a bespectacled blond with dreadlocks and a goatee who reminded her of a self-conscious college student. He would converse briefly though taking off as soon as he heard Cody on the stairwell.

They obviously had not done their homework on the Princess. They did not pick up on the fact that she had been involved in a number of anti-smoking campaigns and had spoken out on behalf of lung cancer victims on numerous occasions. Either that, or the kidnappers might have realized that she was under great stress and was resorting to tobacco to calm her nerves. In any event, they gave her a couple of packs and a lighter she would use to attempt an escape.

She had been given a nail file which she had used throughout the week to cut a hole in the bottom of her mattress. She had spent all her waking time in prayer that morning, waiting until she could smell the odor of cooked food wafting under the door from downstairs. They had left her door unlocked, allowing her to use the bathroom in the hallway as they had broken its lock beforehand.

Jennifer said one last prayer before flipping the mattress over and tearing the cotton stuffing out. She then doused it with nail polish remover before throwing the window open wide. She then lit the cotton, watching it burn until the room was filled with smoke which began billowing out the window. She then threw open the door and began racing down the steps.

"Fire! Fire!" she began yelling. "Everybody out! The building's on fire!"

She looked around the parlor area and got her first look at the other four gang members, who stared at her amusedly as she ran for the front door. This was not doing a lot for her confidence, but if the door did not open she could at least try and jump through a window. If she made it outside and could get up and run, it was going to take a whole lot to catch Jennifer with a head start in a foot race.

She yanked open the door and was stunned at the sight of Baxter Cody, blocking her way with arms folded like Superman.

"Nice try, Princess," he grinned tautly before throwing a snapping right that dropped her unconscious to the floor. Cave Cat Sammy and Joe Coolio scurried over and lifted her off the carpet, carrying her back upstairs to her smoke-filled room.

To his dismay, Cody would find out that the Princess' gambit paid off in spades. Approximately twenty three thousand miles above the earth, Homeland Security's Chernobyl satellite detected the smoke and reported it to the CIA a half hour before Jon and Slash pulled up to the isolated farmhouse thirty miles from Belfast. Fritz Hammer had contacted Homeland Security that morning and got in touch with Sandra Flores, the Chief of Security of DHS. Sandra, in turn, contacted the Chernobyl team in hopes of gathering more information as to the possible whereabouts of Princess Jennifer in the Belfast area. The tranquility of the area in the early morning hours made it easy for them to detect anything out of the ordinary within a fifty mile radius around Belfast.

Chernobyl was one of America's best-kept secrets, its biggest weapon in its war against global terrorism. Disguised as a weather satellite, it had the ability to locate an insect anywhere on the planet given its coordinates. They spotted the smoke, determined its origin to be from the farmhouse, and used the most sensitive sensor probes on earth to estimate that there were seven people inside the building. The information was called in to Jon and Slash at the Tara Lodge, and they hightailed it out to Port Muck after being given precise directions.

"What's it looking like?" Jon radioed the surveillance helicopters hovering miles overhead, peering through the cloud cover in order to avoid detection.

"Area appears secure. We've got our backup in place. Master Blaster says it's a go."

Jon pulled up in their BMW in front of the farmhouse gate and the agents exited the vehicle. They shut the car door, and as if on cue, two stonefaced men stepped out onto the front porch of the green roofed, two-story frame building.

"Help you guys?" Baxter Cody called from the porch.

"Kinda got lost out here. We're looking for the golf course," Jon called over, opening the front gate.

"Don't open that gate," Cody warned. "We got attack dogs."

"What?" Jon put his finger behind his ear, calling across the thirty-foot clearing. "Can't hear you."

"Are you deaf!" Robert Ramjet yelled. "He said don't come in here!"

"Take the marbles out of your mouth!" Slash bellowed.

At once the UDA men drew automatic weapons and began firing at the CIA agents. Jon and Slash high-jumped the fence and rolled toward their vehicle, which was punched full of bullet holes by the gunmen. They pulled their pistols and began firing back as the agents could hear the roaring of an engine behind the house. The UDA men had rolled Jennifer in a carpet and carried her out the back door, throwing her in their panel truck before spinning around to the front of the building. Cody and Ramjet dodged bullets in sprinting across the lawn and diving into the opened panel doors.

"I smell gas!" Slash yelled as he took cover behind the bullet-riddled BMW. "They must've hit the gas tank!"

"Shit!" Jon snarled. "Try and hit their tires if you get a shot!"

At once they could hear the growling of heavy vehicles up the road from whence they came. Their hearts leaped in their chests as they saw a convoy of military trucks racing over the hillside, the silhouette of a helicopter descending from the clouds.

"All right!" Jon yelled. "These bastards are toast!"

"They're coming in from all sides!" Slash spotted yet another truck speeding over the hillside on his left. "This looks like checkmate!"

"Hold on," Jon stared at the black van bouncing in from the west. "I don't think that's a military vehicle."

"Throw down your weapons and put your hands in the air!" a voice blared from loudspeakers on the hovering Apache gunship.

Everyone on the field watched in fascination as the black truck swerved and came to a halt on the grassy knoll.

"All right, gentlemen," Berlin Mansfield got out of the vehicle, "it's show-time."

Jon and Slash watched in apprehension as the six men in black climbed out of the armored van carrying RPG-7 grenade launchers. The leader fired a rocket at the Apache helicopter, hitting it squarely in the tail section. At once the chopper began billowing black smoke and going into a tailspin, doing its best to find an emergency landing behind a nearby drumlin. Three other men stepped up, took aim and fired at the three armored trucks closing in along the road. The grenades slammed into the front ends of each truck, blowing the vehicles off the road and flipping them off onto the meadow. The squad of riflemen scrambled to escape the troop carrier, spreading out to spray automatic fire onto the attackers. Only the other two men fired their grenades, and they exploded in spreading gas throughout the area. The gas dispersed immediately upon hitting the air, taking on an acrid black cloudiness that stung the eyes and burned the lungs. The soldiers were forced to fall back as all three vehicles were surrounded by the dark mist.

The kidnappers' van took advantage of the distraction to streak north along the country road, hitting ninety miles an hour as it came parallel to the wreckage along the intersection. The soldiers were unable to recover from the gas attack long enough to fire upon the escaping van. Jon and Slash watched helplessly as the van disappeared over the drumlin. The occupants of the black truck hopped back into their vehicle and crossed the knoll back to whence they came.

"You mean you aren't going after them?" Chuck Chop stared balefully at the white truck they believed to be containing the Princess heading in the opposite direction.

"All good things come to those who wait," Berlin Mansfield smiled as Al the Cat negotiated the drumlins at breakneck speed. "Now everyone has an idea of our capabilities. I believe both the kidnappers and the British Army will be seeing this whole thing from a completely different perspective after this."

"You know, this isn't a friggin' paintball game," Chuck fumed. "You're screwing with the British Army, the SAS, MI6 and god knows who else. You're not gonna be happy until one of us gets killed."

"I'm quite sure you want to see what's in the red canisters, not to mention the black ones. We can drive you to the airport if you like, but I'll bet your curiosity will get the best of you and it'd just be a waste of time and gas."

"He's not going nowhere," Kurt the Bruiser grunted, staring out the window at the smoke from the Apache rising over the hills. "Let's just nail those bastards, let you get your autograph, thank-you kiss or whatever the hell you're after, and get the hell out of Potato Land."

* * *

Once again Jon and Slash found themselves up to their necks in red tape as Army vehicles and helicopters arrived to control the damage at the contact point. The teammates accompanied Mark O'Shaughnessy on the flight to Lisburn, where they were transported to Thiepval Barracks which served as the Belfast Regional Command center. O'Shaughnessy was livid in realizing that they had come within minutes of intercepting the kidnappers, and even more so in suspecting Berlin Mansfield of having ambushed the convoy and crippling his helicopter.

"The only ones in the world with that capability are the Russians, the Chinese, and Mansfield," Mark fumed as Jon and Slash sat in his office after he returned from getting a laceration on his arm treated. "And you can be damned sure that the Russkies and the Chinks aren't coming at me on my home field to prevent me from intercepting kidnappers!"

"I just don't see how I can give my people positive confirmation that it was Mansfield," Jon was doubtful. "Okay, maybe the gas angle works out, but how do we know whoever it was didn't get it from the Russians or the Chinese? We haven't ruled out the possibility of the IRA being involved, and we know they've got strong connections to the PLO. We don't know if it was the IRA or the UDA who snatched the Princess. Nobody's claimed responsibility or made any demands yet. The IRA could've easily sent that intercept team out to either take a UDA team out or to back up their own guys."

"The IRA stands to lose everything on a play like that," Mark insisted. "They're the main beneficiary of this entire peace process. If this thing goes through, they've got guaranteed reserved seats in Parliament, automatic deferments for hundreds of imprisoned terrorists, unprecedented sociopolitical currency, you name it. You think they'd take a chance on getting caught with their britches down on a cowboy move like that? If that damned satellite of yours would've given me a heads up, I would've personally sent them to hell with a rocket of my own."

"Which satellite is that, Colonel?" Slash smirked.

"That piece of shite you've got flying around up there that doesn't exist," Mark retorted.

"I know you and Fritz Hammer go back a long ways," Jon exhaled. "I know that more than anything else, he wants this to be the one that puts you in the Hall of Fame. The problem is that I can't afford to put my imprimatur on something as shaky as this. Just because you got Darth Vader dancing with Princess Leia at the Peacenik Ball a few nights ago doesn't necessarily mean they beamed him down with his poison gas cans to go rescue the chick. Don't forget, I was the last of the good guys who got to see her, and the bad guys kicked me in the face. I can go either way with them being IRA or UDA, but even today I haven't seen anything that looks like Berlin Mansfield."

"Don't forget, the IRA and the UDA aren't the only prime time players out there," Slash pointed out. "You've got the INLA[1], the Official IRA, plus a ton of UDA spinoffs on the other side. Any one of them could have gotten the Russians to slip them some gas cans through the PLO to do some beta testing out here for them."

"All right, you go back and tell Fritz and the rest of your bosses you don't think it's Mansfield," Mark growled as he headed out the door. "Good luck with your fishing expedition on Ormeau Road. At least I'll know where to find you the next time the bastard turns up."

"Hey, this is your office," Jon called after him.

"Him and Fritz, eh?" Slash chuckled as they got up to leave. "Match made in heaven."

One of the British Army soldiers watched the Americans leaving Mark's office, and waited until they were out of sight before calling out on a secured line.

"Uh huh."

"Yanks leaving. Same ones identified at the Europa."

---

1. Irish National Liberation Army

"I'll tell Grandma."

The line went dead.

* * *

The agents made arrangements to pick up another vehicle from Enterprise at Belfast international Airport before driving down to Ormeau Road before sunset. It had been a long brutal day and they were both burned out. They decided to touch bases with Deryl before heading back to the hotel and calling it a night. Most likely if Deryl was up to grabbing a pint, they would find it within themselves to oblige. They both enjoyed his company and would be able to stand an hour or two of girl-watching if the occasion presented itself.

"How do you like that?" Jon grumbled as they pulled up in front of the storefront. "Closed on schedule. Hope he had a hot date."

"It's not like he's selling potato pancakes," Slash allowed. "You're not gonna have people standing in line with thirty grand waiting to buy a bike in this economy."

"All the more reason to hang around for an extra ten minutes or so to see if anyone shows up," Jon switched off the engine. He turned to see Slash staring incredulously at him before they both shared a laugh. They got out of the replacement BMW and headed for the darkened store, letting themselves in and heading to the back office.

"I wonder how much crap O'Shaughnessy's gonna be shoveling onto Fritz before we check in tomorrow," Slash mused, finding a pint of cognac in the top drawer of the desk where he had left it.

"I'm wondering if they managed to keep it out of the papers," Jon replied, stretching out in a seat in front of the desk. "That Apache was fuming big-time out there. They had to be able to see it from Larne. Plus those explosions must have shaken some furniture all around Port Muck. With the IRA and the UDA denying they know anything about the Princess, the public's bound to think this had to do with the kidnapping."

"Like I said, there's a lot more teams in this league besides the IRA and the UDA," Slash disagreed. "People may think it was just another terrorist attack. Besides, the Brits're gonna spin this anyway they like. That's why I won't be surprised if Fritz buys that Mansfield angle hook, line and sinker."

"I don't give a damn who's behind it. As long as we nail someone and bring that chick back in one piece, it might as well be Mansfield. I'm getting sick of seeing Irish people beating on Irish out here. It's repulsive. These are the best people on earth. Why are they bringing their kids up in an atmosphere like this?"

"I don't know about the best people on earth, but maybe that cousin of yours might get them some brownie points with that holy-rolling operation next door."

"Go figure," Jon shrugged as Slash took a swig of cognac and passed him the bottle. "His Dad and his Grandpa used to be Bible-thumpers, but I never expected him to try it. You never know, they say you catch more bees with honey. Hey, it works in prison, who's to say it can't work out on the street?"

They heard a commotion at the front door, and Jon hopped up to see if it was Deryl. He was bemused at the sight of two men in black suits and ties closing the door behind them.

"Good evening," he strolled out onto the floor where three Titans sat across the walkway from three Harleys. "We're closed for the evening. The manager'll be back in the morning. I can take a message if you like."

"Yeah, I got a message for someone," the first man grunted. They were big burly guys with shaved heads who looked like they just got paroled. "You the owner here?"

"One of them. Something I can help you with?"

"I had people come out here Saturday. They got the impression you were opening up a Caddy shack here. You fellows aren't from around here, are ye?"

"Not originally. How could you tell the difference between a Caddy or a Proddy shack?"

"Around here we can tell by the color of the streak down their back. Sometimes it's green but most of the time it's yellow."

"I'll tell you, pal, the only green I give a shit about is the color of money. If you don't have any, you're wasting my time."

"How about the golf course? Know anyplace around here we can find a good eighteen holes?"

"I don't know. You interested in me tearing you a new one?"

"That's the trouble with these returned empties," the second man growled. "Big talk, no action."

"You guys looking for some action?"

"Sure," the first man snarled as both men drew pistols from their shoulder holsters. Jon beat them to the draw and put three shots into the chest of the first man. The second one fired a volley which caused Jon to leap for cover behind one of the bikes. He returned fire and put holes in a couple of the Harleys, causing the gas tanks to spurt fuel onto the floor.

"That's your arse, Yank," the gunman called over, hiding behind a Titan. "Toss your gun and c'mon out, and I'll let ye live. Otherwise I'll fire a shot and blow ye to hell."

"Think this is a movie?" Jon yelled back as Slash appeared in the doorway, having stuffed a piece of paper into his cognac bottle. "A bullet's not gonna do shit."

"This is," Slash said, firing shots into the display window before holstering his pistol and producing a lighter. Jon got up and dove out the window as Slash lit the paper and threw the bottle across the room.

The showroom exploded in a cloud of flames as the motorcycles' gas tanks created secondary explosions. Jon and Slash covered their faces as window glass sprayed the side street. The heat was so intense that they instinctively patted their heads to make sure their hair had not caught fire. Jon holstered his Glock just as an RUC patrol car careened around the corner and screeched to a halt before them. They were ordered to their knees, then down on their faces before they were cuffed and dragged to the police vehicle. There they remained with guns held against their heads before the fire trucks and ambulances arrived.

They knew this was going to be another long, long night.

Chapter Five

Eddie Doherty was beside himself with anger the next morning as bad news seemed to await at every turn. There had been no word from the kidnap team until the wee hours of the morning. Baxter Cody contacted Delmore Merrick and informed him the team was moving west to elude the British Army. They were on the move but would need to have a rendezvous arranged and a safe house prepared in the next few hours. He also found out that both his enforcers had been killed in the explosion at the American Choppers showroom. He was also in desperate need of a smuggling team to substitute for Cody's squad in moving the London heroin shipment at the Belfast shipyards to their Dublin distributors.

He was on the phone all morning trying to control the damage with limited results. He called his media connections and ordered them to establish a link between the Americans and yesterday's incidents. Their spin doctors came up with a concept of the American Mercenaries, who had not only witnessed the Princess kidnapping but had been hired by corporate interests to rescue Jennifer. It was they who were involved in the military attack of the farmhouse at Port Muck, and the bombing of the motorcycle dealership on Lower Ormeau Road. The Mercenaries, they insisted, were endangering the citizens of Ulster with their capers and should be deported immediately.

The heroin shipment was assigned to G.W. Mc Lintock, a battalion lieutenant on Shankill Road known for his brutal reputation as a UDA enforcer. Doherty was leery of Mc Lintock's smuggling abilities but knew that he was a capable gunman who would die before allowing the shipment to fall into the wrong hands. He made contact with Mc Lintock's sergeant and ordered them to pick up the contraband this evening and drive it to Dublin before daylight.

The remaining problem was the storefront church next door to the charred remains of the American Chopper showroom. Miraculously it remained untouched by the blast, and was gaining support from both sides of the community by each passing day. The man they called the Missionary had opened a pantry and was giving out bread that was donated by local supermarkets. People came by to pray every morning, and he was becoming increasingly vociferous in speaking out against sectarian violence and the kidnapping of the Princess. Doherty decided that Deryl Lee Kilmarnoch had to go.

"This is going to turn into a bonehead play, Ed," Delmore Merrick sipped his third Irish coffee of the morning at the social club. "The people in the neighborhood love this fellow. He's not doing any harm. As a matter of fact, he's doing things we should be handling with that pantry of his. Maybe you should be donating to him instead of trying to run him off."

"Are you blootered already?" Doherty thundered. "Did you forget what this thing of ours is all about in the first place? We thrive on this sectarian crap. Once the Troubles are over, there's no further need for a UDA. I agree with that eejit Baxter on that point, if the peace talks are successful, we're history. That bastard out there is sabotaging our organization. You have him moved out or I'll do it for you."

"And who'll you send for what reason? Baxter and his men are out there dodging half the British Army. Murphy and Bernard are dead. And now you've got Mc Lintock's crew making deliveries to Dublin for you."

"So you don't have anyone else qualified to do this work for me?" Doherty stared at him.

"It's not a question of qualifications, Edward. It's a question of getting made and having to leave Ulster. Whoever takes this man out will bear the mark of Cain for it."

"All right, then," Doherty grunted. "I'm sending Red October."

"What?" Delmore asked incredulously. "Don't you think killing the man will be bad enough?"

"There'll be no more Mercenaries or Missionaries on this side of town on my watch," Doherty assured him. "The only thing American I'll tolerate around here will be tourist money they'll be shelling out to see what's left of that showcase and that holy-rolling joint when I'm done with it."

* * *

That evening, a white panel truck rolled onto an abandoned property just outside Londonderry after a long day of avoiding roadblocks and dodging aerial surveillance flights. Cave Cat Sammy crept up to the farmhouse and found the door left open as planned. He signaled to the others, and his teammates and their captive rushed into the building after parking in the rear beneath the cover of low-hanging tree branches.

"I smell something good, fellas," Victor Charlie called out as he lit a lantern that had been set on the kitchen table. Dan Muni pulled the ski mask with the stitched eyeholes off Jennifer's head and cut the tape off her wrists. She promised to behave and they, in turn, let her out of the carpet she had been wrapped in. Baxter switched on his flashlight and spotted the bags of food that had been left behind for them. He began handing the Styrofoam containers of fish and chips out, and the others began wolfing the food down as fast as they got their hands on it.

"Gee, I guess we didn't realize how hungry we were," Jennifer smiled shyly, wiping grease from her hands and mouth once Cody finally passed out the napkins and utensils. They all broke into a hearty laugh, the utensils of little use at that point. They had eaten the food with their fingers after not having had a decent meal since the gun battle on the previous day.

"Okay, Princess, you come with me," Cody tried not to grin. "The rest of you guys, check the perimeter. Made sure all the shades are drawn and no lights visible from the outside. Get the mess cleaned up, I don't want to be putting my paperwork down in grease stains on that table. I'll take care of our guest here, you guys get some rest and be ready to move at 0400."

"Four o'clock?" Roger Ramjet exclaimed. "We just got here!"

"There's a warehouse in town that'll afford us better protection. It's in a friendly neighborhood and we'll have better coverage in case the Brits move in against us. Not to mention those two Yanks and whoever was in that armored truck that knocked out that entire military unit." Jennifer followed him into the back area, and there was a small windowless room with a cot just as his connections had told him.

"Listen, Cody, I really need to take a shower," she entreated him.

"Okay, but don't forget. You screw up again and make any more stupid moves, you'll spend the rest of this operation chained to a post or rolled up in a carpet. You saw what we're dealing with out there. Those bastards'll blow us all to kingdom come and ask questions later."

"My Mum didn't raise any dummies," she assured him. "I'm not planning to be returned to Buckingham Palace in a bucket or a box."

"All right," he relented. "There's soap and towels and a candle and matches in there. I'll put a chair against the door. When you're finished you knock and I'll let you out."

"Yes sir, lieutenant!" she stood at attention and gave him a salute.

"Smart arse," he shook his head as she disappeared into the bathroom.

As hard as he tried, it was proving exceedingly difficult not to fall under Jennifer's charm.

* * *

Around that same time, the elderly women and housewives who had come down to A Place to Pray noticed the arrival of an exceedingly attractive young woman at the storefront church. She had long red hair and striking blue eyes, and an hourglass figure that revealed her beautiful legs in a tasteful black business suit. She sat in the back of the church and lowered her head in prayer for almost a half hour before Deryl gave his sermon.

"Well, as you all know by now, I'm not much of a preacher," Deryl spoke into the microphone hooked up to a stand and a small amplifier. "I just want to thank everyone for coming and joining with us to make our voices louder and stronger in praying to our Father in heaven. Now, we all were greatly shocked and saddened by the catastrophe that occurred next door last night, and we pray for the families of those two men who were killed there. I guess some of you know that I was employed there, and the police are still trying to find out who was in there and how the explosion occurred. I just thank the Lord that our sanctuary here was not destroyed, and that no one was here when it happened."

"Friends, this is just another example of why this senseless violence here in Northern Ireland must end once and forever. My cousin, the fellow who owned the place next door, once said that the idea of Irish killing Irish was repugnant. I could not agree with him more. They call Ireland a place of terrible beauty, and I ask myself why it should be described in such a way. This is the ethnic homeland of some of the most wonderful, talented, motivated and spiritual people in history. It is said that the prophet Jeremiah migrated here thousands of years ago and brought the blessings of the Israelites to our Celtic ancestors. This is the land of Cuchulainn, of Jonathan Swift, of James Joyce, of leprechauns and banshees, myths and wonders. How could we have ever let it fall into the state of confusion and strife that we live in? How can we accept what happened next door as just another incident, just another unfortunate event that we deal with on a daily basis?"

"Brothers and sisters, this conflict has grown so grotesque and unmanageable that the Princess of Edinburgh has been kidnapped and remains missing for no other reason than having the temerity to believe she could make a difference. The military and law enforcement have no clue as to where she is, or if she is even alive or dead. This is yet another act of senseless violence, another example of how the misguided actions of angry men accomplish nothing but injure our nation and alienate our people. You and I can set an example here. You and I can make a difference. We can go to our knees in worship of our God in the spirit of peace and repentance, and show our neighbors across Belfast and throughout Northern Ireland that violence is no longer an acceptable answer. We will have peace, for we will accept nothing else."

At the end of the service, he stood at the doorway and bade everyone farewell as they left the building. One of the last was the beautiful stranger, who looked into his eyes as she shook his hand.

"I've seen too many people die in this conflict," she said softly. "I'll be back here and join your group in praying for an end to this."

"Thank you, sister," he patted her hand, fighting his male instincts in admiring her stunning beauty. "We'll look forward to seeing you again."

She would be returning much sooner than he thought, in a manner he would have never imagined.

* * *

A couple of hours later in a tenement across town, Kevin Moore was returning to his apartment after an evening of gambling and drinking at a UDA social club on Shankill Road. He was a UDA lieutenant in charge of a squad that was well-known for their drug dealing and blackmarket activities along the outskirts of the Catholic West Side. They sold narcotics to Catholics and stolen goods from Catholic neighborhoods to their Protestant customers at bargain prices. Moore was despised and envied by many as a result but well-respected as a money earner and a man not to be trifled with.

The tenement was in a rundown area and was in need of refurbishment. Yet once one walked into Moore's apartment, they were greatly surprised and impressed by its luxury. Thick rugs covered its parquet floors, and expensive wallpaper and drop ceilings were enhanced by chandeliers, exotic lamps and oil paintings along the walls. The exquisite Victorian furniture included a number of priceless antiques, and it could be seen that Moore was a man of excellent taste.

He switched on the light in the foyer, and walked into the living room where he was startled by the silhouette on a man seated in his recliner. He started to reach for his revolver in its holster beneath his suit jacket but heard the ominous jacking of automatic pistols around the room, causing him to freeze.

"Good evening, Mr. Moore. I apologize for the intrusion, but there is a matter of urgency that brings me here."

"Who the hell are you? How'd you get in here?"

"My name is Berlin Mansfield, not that it will do you any good. My friends and I were the ones who intercepted that convoy in Port Muck that nearly captured your associates. The press made it seem that your friends outwitted the troops and the American Mercenaries, but we all know better. At any rate, you have no chance of escaping, so take a seat on the couch, if you will."

Moore saw three men in opposite corners around the room and realized they had the drop on him. He slowly sat down on the couch, his mind racing in figuring how to get out of this mess.

"What do you want?"

"I need truthful answers, and I have no time whatsoever to waste here. You must tell me exactly what I want or suffer the consequences. Where are the kidnappers?"

"What?"

"Please, Mr. Moore, don't attempt to insult my intelligence. I know you are the district leader in this area and that you are providing backup to the logistical support units along your network. I need to know what city they are headed to and the last place they reported from."

"Look, fellow—Mr. Mansfield—the people who did this thing acted on their own without the approval of anyone in the network you're referring to. They're out there trying to find their way out of this mess they've made. I don't know where they are, and if I did I'd be on my way out there to make them put that woman out on the nearest highway."

"If you will not give us a hand here, then we will take it. Chuck, remove Mr. Moore's right hand."

He could feel a pistol at the back of his head before a plastic bag was thrown over it. His screams were muffled as he was shoved onto the Persian rug on his hands and knees. A boot stomped against his left side, sending him sprawling to his right as his arm was stretched across the floor. He felt something being wound around his forearm before the impact and an indescribable pain in his right wrist.

"Now then," Mansfield's voice was as if coming from miles away as he began to black out from lack of oxygen. "Once you come to, we'll let you see what your lack of cooperation has cost you before I ask you again. I hope we can get this over with as soon as possible for your sake as well as mine."

Chuck Chop put Kevin Moore's right hand up on the massive dining table, waiting for its owner to give Berlin Mansfield the answers he was looking for.

It was a couple of hours after the Mansfield Gang left the apartment on the way to Londonderry that another black panel truck was also on its way out of Belfast. The Mc Lintock crew had picked up a duffel bag containing twenty-five kilos of heroin that would have a street value of two million pounds after processing. They left the Belfast Customs House in short order, having taken possession from four hard-eyed British gangsters who were anxious to create a distance between themselves and the illegal shipment. Mc Lintock expected to complete the 171-kilometer drive to Dublin in a couple of hours, and spend the night carousing before renting rooms and returning in the morning.

They were in sight of the M1 motorway when they saw three black compact trucks careening up on either side of them. The first truck streaked ahead and cut in front of them before they would see red lasers beaming through the windows of both sides of their van. The six-man crew saw riflemen leaning out the windows of both vehicles on either side of them as a bullhorn ordered them to pull off the road.

"Aw reet," McLintock ordered them. "It's gotta be the peelers. Don't forget, we know nothing about what's inside the bag, we were paid to pick it up and drop it off. You don't say a feckin' word until our solicitors arrive."

The UDA men took the nearest exit, ending up along the access road overlooking the River Lagan. They were surrounded by masked gunmen with Uzis who searched the truck and confiscated the duffel bag.

"Yer not the peelers, are ye?" Mc Lintock snarled as he and his men were disarmed and forced to their knees.

"Nay, we're the Evil Mothers, here to rid the streets of this poison yer pumpin' into our community," one of the men told them.

The Mothers Against Drug Dealers were an IRA splinter group that had launched a campaign against narcotics gangs across Northern Ireland. They were known to have kneecapped dealers in Catholic neighborhoods and had less tolerance for Loyalist traffickers. Mc Lintock and his crew watched as a man in a suit and tie emerged from one of the vehicles, followed closely by three men with an expensive videocamera, audio recorder and lighting equipment.

"Get some closeups of those bastards for the telly," the man with the suit ordered. "We also want some clear shots of the contraband."

McLintock and his men squinted in the glare of the spotlights as they were filmed before the duffel bag was opened and the kilos also caught on tape. They watched on in apprehension as the bag was carried over to the railing along the promenade overlooking the river.

The gangsters stared in shock as the man in the suit stood before the camera, reciting a statement about the MADD's mission and how they were relentlessly campaigning against drugs in every neighborhood in Ulster. With that, the camera shifted to where the kilos were taken out from the bag and slit open with knives, the heroin carried by the wind in billowing clouds across the Belfast harbor.

Chapter Six

The video was sent to the BBC and posted on the Internet where it went viral on You Tube. The first broadcast was televised at 6AM and was played every half hour on the news programs. Eddie Doherty was beside himself with anger, bellowing in a rage before and every replay he could find on the cable channels at the social club.

"Do you see that!" Eddie yelled, his face turning red as he shook his fist at the TV screen. "Those bastards dumped my heroin! That's my product being tossed right in the feckin' river!"

"That's what you said the last time they showed it, and it ended up the exact same way. Do you think if they show it on a different channel there may be a different ending?"

A couple of the gunmen tried to keep from snorting and chortling, and as they turned away from Doherty, he weaved before Merrick while trying to catch his breath.

"You," he pointed his finger at Merrick's face. "This is your fault. If you had sent Cody's men to make that pickup instead of Mc Lintock, this would have never happened."

"Cody's men are on the run from the British Army. I told you we were going to have to send Mc Lintock. No one expected him to get hijacked by the Evil Mothers."

"I know what happened, I was here, remember? Now we've got two million pounds worth of product floating in the river! How the hell am I gonna sort this out with Billy Belfast? What makes you think they're not gonna send a hit squad down here looking for their money?"

"There are no guarantees in this business. You know it and they know it. I'll talk to Billy if you like."

"What? Are you running this crew now? You're gonna negotiate with Billy?"

"Give it a rest, Edward. The shipment was lost and we have to decide what to do with the hostage. We're not accomplishing anything sitting around here blowing off steam."

"I didn't give an order to kidnap anyone! If he was going to do anything he should have blown her feckin' head off! You go in, boom-boom-boom, it's all over. You don't bag the strumpet and take her on a joyride all over Ulster. Where are those eejits now?"

"We think they're in Londonderry. Only we may have a problem. Someone broke into Kevin Moore's house and killed him. His housekeeper notified the RUC, and now MI6 is all over it. We've got word Mark O'Shaughnessy showed up. There's talk that the terrorist, Berlin Mansfield, is involved somehow."

"Berlin Mansfield? Who the bloody hell is that?"

"He's that guy who got chased out of Serbia for war crimes a few years ago and turned up in Rwanda," Eddie Mulvahill called over from the bar. "There was a bunch of shite on the telly about him after that. They call him the Golden Terror. They say he's the second most wanted man in the world after Osama Bin Laden. There were rumors on the Internet that he was involved in that bombing in London a couple of weeks ago. You know, where that Al Qaeda guy got killed in that restaurant. He's a professional terrorist, though. He kills for money. He wouldn't be in on this unless somebody put up a ton of it to bring him in."

"Hold on," Doherty sat down across from the silver-haired Merrick. "First we got these Yanks sticking their nose in our business. Now you've got this Berlin Mansfield, not to mention Mark O'Shaughnessy and the whole feckin' British Army. What in the hell are we getting out of this? Why is Cody not dumping that bitch's body out on the street and being done with this?"

"Think of what you're saying," Merrick lit a cigarette. "Do you think making a martyr out of her will improve things? They'd tear this country apart brick by brick to find her killers. Plus the whole world would be sticking their noses in here trying to push that peace treaty through. We need to come out with some kind of statement, acknowledge that we got the woman and what the reasoning was to snatch her in the first place."

"You're the one who gave Cody the nod, you read those stupid reports of his. You know why he did it, so have someone go tell them!"

"I think you'll need to send some proof of life along with it," Mulvahill suggested. "If you send a statement with proof she's alive, it might give the boys a breather. The Brits might hold back a bit if they know she's being held for some cockamamie political reason."

"All right, geniuses, let me ask this," Doherty signaled the bartender to bring him a cup of coffee.

"If you've got this high-rolling terrorist and these American Mercenaries racing Mark to find this hussy, they must know she's alive and well somewhere, don't you know? They're not gonna be blowing each other to hell like they did in Port Muck trying to recover a stiff."

"All right, keep playing mind games," Merrick blew a stream of smoke away from the table. "Only we've lost three men already, along with two million pounds of product. I think we'd better start planning on making a deal while we still have something left to deal with."

* * *

Mark O'Shaughnessy paced the floor at Kevin Moore's apartment, comparing notes with RUC officers and MI6 agents at he peered at the totem left behind by the Mansfield Gang just hours before.

"This is the kind of thing he did in Rwanda," Mark growled as he looked in at the dining room table. Moore's head sat on top of the table, his hands propped up so that the fingers covered its mouth. The scene was remarkably tidy as if the parts had been washed off to cause the least amount of leakage. "He left us a message. He's telling us he got the information he wanted from this fellow. There's no doubt the UDA's involved in this. A man like Mansfield doesn't waste time, he's living day to day. He knew who to look for and where to find him. This fellow Moore told him where to look next. Mansfield's after that girl, and we have to figure out who's paying him and why."

"The problem we got is the UDA are like first cousins to the Orange Order, and the Order is everywhere," the female RUC detective pointed out. "We've got people throughout the Constabulary that belong to the Order. We've got no guarantee of confidentiality anywhere if it concerns the UDA, and it's a one-way street. And that works both ways. If these terrorists start targeting UDA members for information about the kidnapping, there's no way we can protect them all. The other problem is, no one seems to know anything about this. Even our top supergrass agents got no wind of this. Nobody saw this coming, and no one's hearing anything about the Inner Council's reaction to it."

"The UDA's full of stone cold killers who have no problem with scenes like this," the MI6 agent shook his head. "Those terrorists may have bitten off more than they can chew coming in here and playing the role like this. If the UDA gets hold of them before we do, this may well be a parlor trick compared to what payback can be like."

"Did you see what Mansfield did to my chopper the other day?" Mark squinted. "Those bastards could bring it to the PLO if they had to. The UDA is small potatoes for Mansfield. We need to start outguessing him and intercepting him before he makes any more moves like this. You people aren't letting the press in on this, are you?"

"It's not a question of us letting them in on it," the detective replied. "This man was a brigadier in West Belfast. There's no way you can keep this out of the papers. The word's probably out on the street right now as sure as we're standing here. The problem is if anyone manages to tie Mansfield in with any of the Republican groups. That could easily lead to a major outbreak of sectarian violence."

"That's the way it works out here," a second RUC detective came over. "It's not a matter of what the groups do against each other. It's about what they do to the people in the communities. I don't think any of us give a damn if all those militants send each other to hell. We're worried about the poor souls who are trapped in those neighborhoods with no place to go."

"All right, here's the deal," Mark decided. "I want you to round up this fellow's crew and find out what he might have possibly told Mansfield. We need to head him off, set a trap wherever he's going. We need to squeeze the brigadiers, the Inner Council members, and find out who was most likely to have ordered the kidnapping. We also need to let the communities know that those militants aren't doing them any favors. We'll put all of Ulster in lockdown if we have to. Mansfield's made his move, now it's ours. We need to show these bastards who really controls Northern Ireland."

Jon Stevens was beginning to wonder just who that might be. He reported the incident at American Choppers to Fritz Hammer, who put a lot of weight on his sources for information. It turned out that Murphy and Bernard had a lifetime of criminal activity behind them. They were suspected of being members of the UDA but it remained unconfirmed by the RUC. The authorities had no explanation as to why the men had pulled guns on the dealership owners other than the sectarian slurs Jon and Slash had reported to the police.

They met Mark at Belfast International Airport where they accompanied him on a helicopter flight to the Waterside area of Londonderry. It was known as a Protestant stronghold on the East Side, located across the Foyle Bridge from the center of town. They arrived at Clooney Barracks that afternoon, where they set up a command center to plot their strategy should the Mansfield Gang make a move along northwest Ulster.

"According to our sources, a large order of hot food, drinks and picnic supplies was sent out to this area from town the other night. It was called in to a Protestant-owned fish and chips spot, and the deliveryman was directed to a rendezvous at the Top of the Hill Park near the Altnagelvin District. The kid who made the delivery got busted a couple of hours later with his friends smoking pot at the park, and he used the info to cut a deal to get off the hook. There were just two men in a car who paid for the food. The RUC called it into us. I'm thinking it may or may not have been dropped off for the kidnappers. That means Mansfield may or may not be onto it," Mark briefed them as they sat in a small office at the barracks poring over the latest reports.

"So that's the best lead we got right now. That's why we flew all the way out here to Derry," Jon grumbled.

"You know, I've been sent here to conduct a classified rescue operation," Mark narrowed his eyes. "It doesn't do at all for me to be flying around with the American Mercenaries, or whatever the tabloids are calling you two."

"Yeah, well, I've already got Fritz Hammer up my ass for that. You've worked with Fritz before. You know he doesn't have a reputation for his kind and gentle patience. So we're hoping that wasn't a food delivery for a bunch of guys roughing it in the countryside, or a couple of jerks deciding to meet the delivery guy halfway to save on gas."

"I like my story better."

"I do too," Slash decided. "So if they're out here, it's probably somewhere here in the Loyalist area."

"That's what I'm figuring. I'm trying to maintain as low a profile as possible, but rest assured I have a lot of plainclothes men on the street on bikes running license plate checks on anything that can comfortably hold over six passengers."

"So we're pretty well spinning our wheels here until either the kidnappers or Mansfield make their move."

"We'll be more than glad to loan you a car so you can join the search."

"Sounds good," Jon smiled over at Slash. "I think I'd rather be cruising around Derry than sitting up here waiting for reports from the traffic cops to come in."

As Jon and Slash headed for the motor pool, Deryl Lee Kilmarnoch was preparing for his nightly service at A Place To Pray. He had warmed up to his task now that he had over fifty people coming by on a daily basis. He opened from seven to ten AM, then closed for lunch and reopened from 1 PM to 4 PM. He then returned from six to nine, when the bulk of his 'parishioners' came by after supper.

Eddie Doherty was adamant that the storefront church disappear as had the motorcycle shop. He saw it as a thorn in his side, especially with what he was perceiving as challenges to his authority as of late. The fact that the Princess kidnapping was ruining his business was just part of it. Losing Murphy and Bernard while the Americans escaped made it worse. Having the heroin shipment confiscated was more than he could tolerate. He wanted there to be no mistake that Eddie the Bull continued to rule East Belfast with an iron hand. This job was to be a work of art.

Deryl was on his knees in prayer at the front of the church shortly after dark. He did not interrupt his worship though he heard the door open and close behind him. Most of the time the visitors found seats and went into their own prayer routine. Very few had much to say to him. It was as if everyone respected each other's privacy and would not let the burdens of their daily lives impose upon this place of meditation and refuge.

The beautiful redhead had returned as she said she would. She saw the preacher on his knees at the makeshift altar rail, his elbows resting atop it as he leaned forward in prayer. She walked very softly up the aisle, purposefully approaching him as she opened her purse. She pulled out her fully-loaded .357 Magnum which was filled with dum-dum slugs. She knew that one of these bullets would enter a man from one side and tear a grapefruit-sized hole at the point of exit. If she emptied the pistol into this man, most likely the podium would appear as an abattoir when the police arrived.

She came up behind him, pointing the barrel at the back of his head and pulling the trigger. She cursed to herself as the Magnum apparently misfired. She fired again, her eyes wide as saucers as she watched the firing pin hit the cylinder to no avail. The gun clicked six times before he turned around and stood up before her.

"This is not what God wants," Deryl said softly, looking into her eyes. "Is this really what you want?"

He put his hands on her shoulders, and at once she dropped her revolver and her purse and sprawled backwards across the carpeted aisle. Her eyes rolled back in her head and she began praying in a foreign tongue, convulsing as if experiencing a seizure. Deryl sank to his knees alongside her and raised his hands in prayer. Soon they were both praying in tongues before Shannon Blackburn rose to her knees. She fell against his chest and sobbed hysterically, confessing her sins to Almighty God.

The congregation began filing in, and on this night these was no sermon. Instead they all worshipped God, led by the handsome young couple huddled together in the front seats.

It was a night that all of Belfast would one day remember.

Mark O'Shaughnessy would have been astounded to find that Princess Jennifer was being held only a few miles from his field headquarters. Baxter Cody and his men were holed up in a vacant warehouse at the Altnagelvin Industrial Estate not far from the A6 Highway. They were out of food by noon and tensions were running high as Cody was delaying another food run. He was warned to minimize his phone calls to avoid traces and kept getting the runaround as the Londonderry Brigade were under enormous pressure from the local Army and RUC.

"What are you planning to do, starve us to death?" Victor complained as the men languished around the dark and dusty warehouse. Making matters worse was the fact that Cody was enforcing noise and light discipline so that they remained in silence and darkness after sunset. "Why don't we just get the hell out of town if it's this damn bad around here?"

"Listen, fellow, you're supposed to be a soldier, so start acting like one!" Cody blazed at him. "We're in this middle of a major operation here, we're not here for your personal convenience! If you were out on the field you wouldn't have the convenience of calling a feckin' restaurant for takeout! You saw what those bastards threw at us in Port Muck. We need to sit tight until it's safe for us to move from here. We're in friendly territory and it's after dark, it can't be much longer before they give us the go-ahead."

"Hey, I'm a team player here. I just don't want us waiting here to get nailed. Why don't you let me go out and do recon and see if I can grab some stuff? Even a loaf of bread, some peanut butter and a six-pack of soda would tide us over, and it wouldn't rouse suspicion. They're not gonna be looking for one guy in a van buying the makings for a peanut butter sandwich."

"Dammit," Cody snarled. He had the Princess upstairs in an office space along with Sammy as her guard. The others were on each side of the building keeping watch. "All right, take Ramjet with you. Get back on Glenshane Road and see if there's anything open near the hospital. You may find something along Clooney Road, but if you see the peelers you turn around and get right back here. Got it?"

"I'm on it."

"All right. You keep your cell phone in hand at all times. If you're intercepted you give me the emergency signal and I'll evacuate this place."

"Yes sir, I got it," Victor's attitude greatly improved as he hurried over to fetch Roger.

"How's everything going up there?" Cody called up to Sammy in the shadows.

"Can I have a word?"

"All right, but make it short," Cody beckoned him. Sammy warned the Princess not to do anything foolish before he trotted down the metal steps from the upper catwalk.

"She's not doing too good, Bax," Sammy said reluctantly. "She's been living in Buckingham Palace, for cripes' sake. She's pretty depressed and she's wondering why we don't at least send out for something to drink. If she gets sick we're gonna have a real problem on our hands."

"Bax?" Dan Muni came rushing over from the other side of the warehouse. "I made contact. I got a number for you to call in three minutes. I think it's gonna be Del."

"Thank god," Cody exhaled. "You saved the number? Gimme the phone."

Cody stared at his watch intently and dialed the phone at exactly 1800.

"Hullo."

"Del. It's Bax."

"Ed's making a move tomorrow night. It'll create a diversion so you can get to Armagh overnight. He and I will be out there to meet you Friday night. Call Rocky Fitzpatrick in the morning for confirmation." The line went dead.

"Well, shite, that was short and sweet," Cody glowered at the phone in his hand.

He was still trying to figure out what to make of the call as Victor and Roger cruised up Highway A6 towards Altnagelvin Hospital. They decided to play it safe and pick up whatever they could from the waiting area in the complex. Victor figured they would get a bunch of change and buy snacks and sodas from the vending machines. If they kept watch on one another in the lobby they could go back and forth and buy enough stuff to fill a couple of sacks. They had all worked security at one time in their lives and knew what a blessing a bag of chips and a can of soda could be to an empty stomach. They just had to be cautious not to arouse suspicion with just two guys buying so much junk food.

"Suppose they have a cafeteria?' Roger wondered. "Think we'll get lucky?"

"Hell, whatcha gonna do, order seven plates to go?" Victor scowled.

"Maybe we could just get ourselves something to eat."

"That'd be pretty cold shite, don't ye think?"

"Hey, there's a van parked along the side road there, slow down. Maybe it's the peelers."

"Right."

Victor slowed down and went into his right lane to avoid the black van on their left. They continued along their way to the hospital but it was enough to arouse the suspicion of the occupants on the van.

"Let's follow those fellows and see where they end up."

"Gotcha, Boss."

Berlin Mansfield's calculations were flawless as he considered the fact that the abductors would most likely wind up near a hospital in a Protestant area in case they needed medical assistance. All they were able to get from Kevin Moore was the fact that the kidnappers were heading to the Londonderry area to escape the dragnet around Belfast. Yet he had already seen the white van from a distance and knew that they would have to stay in areas where trucks of that size would be least obvious. Two men in a truck might be going to pick up an injured comrade at the hospital, or going in for supplies, or possibly running recon. Mansfield had all the time in the world on his hands, so he would see what this van with two men was up to.

They parked across the road from the hospital as Kurt the Bruiser got out from the driver's seat and focused his high-powered binoculars on the entrance. He hooked up one of their devices and took a picture of the two men, then sent it a wireless transmission to a private number in Dundalk.

"Hello?"

"Mike. I thought I'd check and see if you got my message."

"Dammit, Berlin. I told you not to call me here."

"I'm not going to waste precious time calling one of your flunkies. Besides, this is a relay coming and going from Greenland. Even Chernobyl couldn't figure this out in time to do anything about it."

"So you say. What do you want?"

"I asked you already. I need you to do a check on these two. I'm right across the street from them. They may be running errands for the kidnappers. I've got a white van the same size of the one I nearly smoked in Port Muck. They're parked at a hospital. I think it's worth a look."

"All right, I'll get back to you. Don't call here, dammit. MI6 has been here twice. They're threatening me with crap going back twenty years ago. These people are desperate. My people are stuck in gear all over Ulster. The whole country's in lockdown. You call Jimmy Maher like I told you. He'll have your info in about a half hour."

"I can't wait that long."

"Don't call back here!" Mike O'Beirne snapped before the line went dead.

Mansfield was using the IRA chieftain as his lifeline and was suffering considerable abuse in the process. O'Beirne asked Mansfield to stay out of the situation but to no avail. The attack at Port Muck told Mike that Mansfield was not to be denied. He could not fathom why Mansfield continued to risk his life in this situation but realized this might be the Republicans' best hope. If Mansfield rescued the Princess, the peace process could resume and the intolerable heat brought to bear on the IRA would dissipate. He reluctantly agreed to provide what little help he could, but warned Mansfield that the connection would be severed if a single IRA volunteer was arrested.

"Doesn't that friggin' mick realize the favor you're doing him here?" Kurt growled as he kept watch over the hospital entrance. "This whole island's practically under martial law."

"His neck is stretched as far as ours, yet he has no control over the situation whatsoever," Berlin explained. "If they nail him for any one of the charges they have pending against him, he might go away for the rest of his life. As long as we're in country, if they make the one connection he's a goner. Of course, that's all the more reason why he'll want to help us get on our way as soon as he can."

"Okay. I got one of them coming out with a couple of bags. I bet they're picking up supplies. Maybe they got a connection inside slipping them some medicine."

"Perhaps the Princess is under the weather. I suppose we'll have to do something to relieve her discomfort."

"Let's just grab those bastards, make them bring us back to their hideout, rescue that broad and get the hell over to the Continent."

"In time, Kurt. In time."

They waited until the white van pulled out of the hospital parking lot and returned to the industrial park. The black van followed at a safe distance and found a space near a warehouse barely visible from the loading dock where the van parked. There they would wait until daylight to carry out the next step in Mansfield's master plan.

Chapter Seven

Baxter Cody had his men do a perimeter check and was startled to discover the black van parked diagonally across the street from the rear of their warehouse. He quickly called his team together and had trouble controlling himself when Victor told him that they had seen the truck on the roadside last night.

"You didn't think that was worth mentioning?" Cody asked tautly. "You know the SAS is the best special forces unit on the entire planet, they write the book on surveillance tactics. You didn't think it might possibly be them?"

"Geez, Bax, I didn't think anything either," Roger defended his teammate. "You know it could have easily been some gobshite run out of gas."

"Well, I'm not taking the same chance twice," Cody replied. "Pack up and get the Princess. We need to get the hell out of here. We'll go back towards the Caddy area and take our chances. You know the plan, if we get intercepted we'll go to a hostage mode and bargain our way out."

The team bagged their gear and brought Jennifer back down. Her tummy was growling and she slept poorly in a thin blanket in the drafty warehouse. Only by now she was developing a strange sense of bonding with her captors. She realized they were a bunch of scared kids who got themselves in a jam they couldn't find a way out of. She knew she was being held by terrorists though she couldn't tell which side they were on. She could see they were getting terrible support and did not really know where they were heading next. She was cold, hungry, thirsty and tired, but she knew they were in just as bad a shape and she would not cause a ruckus over it.

"Okay, Princess, we're gonna have to do the carpet roll. I'm sorry, but I can't risk the safety of my men. Vic, Rog, you guys tuck her in. Sammy, Dan, Joe, you guys fan out and keep watch on that van. If they make a move on us, take their tires out."

"Can't I sit with you fellows?" Jennifer's eyes grew misty. "I'll be good, I swear."

"Sorry, Jen. Anybody spots that blonde hair of yours with that satellite tracking crap of theirs, it'll be game over."

"Let her wear a ski cap," Sammy said softly. "I'll watch her."

"You've got your orders, soldier," Cody turned away, heading out to the truck. Most of the team began repenting they had ever taken on this mission.

Jennifer wept as she laid down on the carpet, and Vic and Rog rolled her up before carrying out to the truck. Cody started it up and waited until his three gunmen gave him the okay. He signaled them before they pulled back and jumped into the van. Cody made a sharp turn and veered back onto the A6 towards town.

"Here comes trouble," Sammy looked out the rear window through his binoculars. "The black van's on the move, they're coming up behind us."

"Hang on, I'm gonna take them through the graveyard."

Cody took a sharp left and cut down Church Road to Church Brae into the cemetery. Cody gunned the engine and roared through the east gate, burning rubber as they continued along the narrow path. Sammy could see the black van picking up speed and cutting in from Church Brae through the gates. Cody realized this was going to be one of the most crucial escapes of his life. The road twisted and turned, making it extremely difficult to maintain sixty to seventy MPH speeds without skidding off into a row of gravestones. He could see that the pursuers had it no easier, their truck fishtailing as it raced to keep up.

"Open up the back and take out their windshields!" Cody yelled, fighting desperately to keep from going into a tailspin. "I can't even see the way out from where we are!"

Joe Coolio threw open the back doors as Victor opened up with an Uzi on the black van, which had come to within fifty yards of their quarry. He emptied the clip, most of the rounds being sprayed into the wind though three slugs smashed through the glass.

"Sons of bitches," Chuck Chop yelled as a ricocheting shot hit the window frame by his head. "Stop this thing, I can put a rocket up their ass. We're hitting a straight stretch of road, let's do it!"

"No, we'll have to give them another pass," Mansfield decided. "We can't follow them into Derry with bullet holes in our windshield, not just before rush hour. From what Kurt has gotten on the Internet, they'll have their hands full getting past the Butcher's Gate."

"I can stay close enough to give Chuck a shot at the west gate," Kurt insisted as he fought the road, keeping a distance behind the swerving white van.

"If we cause them to crash, the Princess may be harmed," Mansfield replied. "Plus it may do her well to spend a bit more time with those fellows. She'll be that much happier when we come to her rescue."

"What're we gonna do about this windshield?" Kurt asked, cursing as the white van eventually disappeared out the west gate, veering north towards Church Brae en route to the Craigavon Bridge.

"We'll just get a new vehicle. I'm sure we can find ourselves one at the hospital parking lot that should suit our needs."

The Mansfield Gang ruefully watched the van roaring away as they continued north back to the A6 and the hospital complex. Further up the road, they could see a large number of police and emergency vehicles converging at the Lisnagelvin Shopping Center. Passing motorists had been startled by the sound of gunfire at the cemetery and called police, who immediately put out an all-points alert.

Jon and Slash were among the crowd at the Butcher's Gate, a historic landmark which was one of the seven gates providing access through the city walls. The RUC had set up a checkpoint there which had turned into a public spectacle by rush hour. A large number of students came out to heckle the police, who were conducting cursory checks of vehicles large enough to hold more than six passengers. Many wore pig masks, which rankled the police no end. They chanted and yelled every time a vehicle was stopped, and the police would run them off only for them to creep back to the gate and begin demonstrating once more.

"Shit," Slash got an alert on his mobile device. "They've reported gunfire at the cemetery near the shopping center east of here. I think we'd better check it out."

"You better give Mark a call," Jon replied as they gave up their vantage point near a police barricade. "Ten to one he'll be out there as soon as he gets word."

Just as Jon predicted, Mark's helicopter arrived at the hospital within minutes of Jon and Slash's departure from the Gate. It was not long before the abandoned black van was reported on the hospital parking lot. There were three bullet holes in the windshield and two inside the vehicle, but its occupants had long since fled. They ran a check and learned the van had been purchased in Dublin by a man who had been dead since 1944. The truck had been steel-plated by professionals, and Mark had little doubt that it was the team who had attacked his convoy in Port Muck.

"This is Mansfield," Mark assured them as they met on the heliport at the complex a half hour after Cody and his men had slipped into Derry undetected. "He must have come across the kidnappers and broke contact after getting hit. He's toying with them for some reason. With those rocket launchers of his, he could have put this to an end as soon as he got close enough for them to shoot his windshield. He's got all the tools he needs to have taken them out. He's got the RPG's, he's got his gas canisters. He has no doubt he'll be able to pick up their trail again, and he's definitely not afraid of us."

"Why would you say that?" Jon wondered, lighting a Camel after passing one to Slash. "You guys got a rep as the best in the business."

"He knows we don't want to engage him in open combat in a populated area," Mark replied. "It would be an absolute public relations disaster, especially being as close to a peace agreement as we are. He would have every advantage with those weapons of his. There's nowhere in Ulster where we could exchange rocket fire with him, and our troops are not equipped to counter a gas attack. If we reported that he was using such weapons, it could lead to the forced evacuation of any area where he could be operating. This whole thing could disintegrate into chaos."

"So your people aren't going to say a word about Mansfield to the press. How are you going to find him if no one knows you're looking for him?"

"If we start rehashing press releases on that restaurant bombing in London, we can let on he's still in the UK. That will give the media enough incentive to run some features on him. Plus we can imply that he's running with a gang that resembles the Princess kidnappers. That'll have the community looking even harder for six men in a van. There is more than one way to catch rats. We just have to make the best use of our options."

"I just wonder what the Princess would think about all this," Jon scowled. "I think the entire UK would be up in arms if they even thought she was taken near a medical facility. We're taking about this chick who's like a rock star. A bad day for her was probably about breaking a nail. She's being held by desperate men and is probably scared out of her wits. I'm not sure that playing chess with these guys is your best approach."

"Perhaps your public image might prove useful here," Mark suggested. "I know that storefront church of your cousin's is not sitting well at all with some of the movers and shakers in East Belfast. I think if the two of you were seen out there, it might make some of them a bit more anxious to make a deal."

"See, this is what I'm talking about," Jon was nettled. "You just found Mansfield's van with bullet holes put there by the kidnappers. You know they're not going back to Belfast. We should be looking at where they could be headed next. If you put us next to the kidnappers again, it'll draw Mansfield out in the open and you can take them all out in one sweep."

"I've got an idea where they may be going, and that is why I want you in Belfast jerking the Loyalists' chains. I'm going to step on the necks of some of the Republicans sympathizers along the western sectors of Ulster and I don't necessarily want you two there while I'm doing so."

"So what are you planning to do, send in the storm troopers and start putting people in concentration camps?"

"Not exactly, not just yet," Mark smiled tautly. "Let's just say that if Mansfield has any support whatsoever within the Republican community, I expect it to disappear entirely within a very short time."

"You don't think I'm gonna be spinning my wheels down in Belfast while you're up here pulling that shit," Jon was adamant. "I went through the same crap with General Mladic in Serbia. One night we're sitting down drinking beer in Belgrade, and the next thing I know he's bombing the hell out of Srebrenica. I'm not standing still for it. You start violating human rights out here and I'll be on the phone every half hour with my bosses at Langley. You can tell Fritz Hammer I said so but I don't think you will."

"You're not a politician, my friend. You're a spy. You've gotten as close to having your name in the news as I'm sure you want to be. If you start slandering my command down here, I can assure you that your name will appear right alongside mine."

"You go into one Catholic neighborhood with your rubber bullets and fire hoses, and I'll take my chances," Jon and Slash turned to leave. "I'm thinking they'll show up at either Omagh or Armagh. Those are the two most unlikely places for them to be, and as we can see, they're not having a whole lot of luck with the Loyalists. We'll go look around, and if we see anything interesting we'll give you a buzz."

"Sounds good," Mark managed a smile. "Happy hunting."

* * *

As it turned out, Jon would be second-guessing himself for not having taken Mark's suggestion for a long time to come.

The people from both neighborhoods along Lower Ormeau Road who attended A Place To Pray were intrigued by the beautiful redhead who had moved from the back of the church to the front row. Suddenly she had become the preacher's girl Friday, taking on all the tasks that Deryl had no one else around to do. She acted as the usherette, meeting people at the door, escorting them to their pews, handing out flyers and taking the collection. Rumors of the lovely woman at the church were now attracting a goodly number of male guests which raised the number of visitors to nearly a hundred a day.

By now the collections had allowed Deryl to buy two large coffeemakers, which made the storefront even more popular during the morning hours. Workers came in on the way to work for coffee, and their conscience compelled them to stop in at the end of the day to drop money in the basket. People were stopping by to pass the craic at night, and it started to remind the old-timers of how it was back before the Troubles got out of hand. They remembered back when working men from both sides went to the same pubs, back when they didn't throw bricks through your window for crossing the line. If they got the Princess back, and if more places like this opened up, maybe—just maybe— things might go back to the way they used to be.

The only problem was that it reminded the old folks how a whole generation grew up lost in Us and Them. The East Siders held steadfastly to their traditions at all costs, teaching their kids to be like Us even at risk of losing their own identities in the process. It created enmity towards Them, and They were forced to band together in order to survive. The old folks saw how it had affected the lives of their children, and no longer wanted it for their grandchildren. They did not want to leave a legacy of hate behind them unto the third generation. Maybe this place held hope for something better.

News of events transpiring at A Place to Pray hit Newtownards Road like a thunderbolt. Ed Doherty was shocked to hear of the defection of Shannon

Blackburn and decided enough was enough. Delmore Merrick and Eddie Mulvihill warned him against bombing the storefront as the possible collateral damage would be ruinous to the local UDA. He opted instead to put together a four-man team to end the ministry once and for all.

"There's one thing, Ed," the leader of the squad insisted when Doherty offered them the job at the social club. "We'll do the work on the preacher, but we're not shooting at that bitch. Not at a church, not inside it or anywhere around it. She has the demon, and everyone knows it. Plus we'll need enough money to leave Ulster and live comfortably until it's safe to come back."

The Sunday morning service was scheduled for 8 AM so that Catholics could make their own 9 o'clock mass and Protestants could attend the standard 10 AM prayer meeting. The room was nearly full as Shannon took a seat off to Deryl's left behind the pulpit. He had a big smile on his face, his heart overjoyed by the huge turnout.

Shannon had gotten up to switch off the recorded welcoming hymn, and had her back turned as the four men barged through the front door and rushed up the aisle. Women and children screamed before being yanked to the floor as the masked men drew sawed-off shotguns. Deryl stared in astonishment as they began unloading their weapons at him. The buckshot chewed through the pulpit to get to Deryl, hammering him in the chest and catapulting him backwards onto the podium floor. Shannon cursed and swore as she pulled her .357 Magnum from her purse, but Deryl grabbed her wrist and held her tight until the men made their escape.

Baxter Cody and his men learned of the attack days after meeting with Eddie Mulvihill at a safe house outside the city of Armagh. Somehow the kidnappers had eluded the RUC dragnet after the alert was spread throughout Derry once Mansfield's van was discovered. They escaped the city limits and drove south, bypassing the huge military force amassed around Omagh and heading straight down Highway N2 to Armagh.

"Crossing the border into the Republic is out of the question," Mulvihill told him as they met in a barn outside Killylea in Armagh County. "The Garda Siochana's got it all sealed off in case Berlin Mansfield tries to cut across."

"Berlin Mansfield?" Cody wondered.

"He's a mercenary, a German terrorist," Mulvihill pushed a packet across the table set up in the drafty barn. He was dressed in a fedora and a black overcoat, his men waiting outside as they delivered food and blankets to the team that night. "He's the one who came at you in Port Muck and Londonderry. Right now the Brits are more concerned about him than the Princess. They say he used chemical weapons against the convoy in Port Muck. Plus he's got rocket launchers. They're not informing the media because they don't want it to hinder their search for the Princess or cause a panic. They can't keep it secret forever, and that's why we have to act."

"Who the hell's he working for?" Cody opened the envelope and looked at the photos.

"We don't know. The Republicans couldn't possibly afford him, maybe the PLO's bankrolling it. What we know is that the Bull wants this thing over with. You need to make plans to end this thing. He wants the matter terminated, and those are his words."

"What do you mean, terminate the Princess?" Cody asked in disbelief.

"I'm just relaying a message, I don't give a shite one way or another," Mulvihill tried not to be apologetic. "Something for ye to think about, lad. Why were ye giving handwritten reports to a man who does not read? Were ye hoping he would ignore yer reports so you could go ahead and do as ye pleased?"

"No, I wanted him to be able to pass it around so that others could fully understand what we were doing and why we were doing it," Cody insisted.

"Pass it to who, son? Others who do not read? We did not go into this life of ours because we were skilled at reading and writing, and understanding political ideas. You brought something to the table that no one could make heads or tails of. You got your wish and now you must live with the consequences. You've got to get rid of her, boy."

"What are you trying to say?"

"We can't bear the weight any longer. Our RUC connections are running for cover. We're trying to blame it on the Croppies but MI6 found out about Mansfield getting Kevin Moore to rat you out."

"You mean it was this guy Mansfield who killed Kevin?"

"It had to be him. First Kevin got his head taken off, then the next thing we know you've got Mansfield on your tail. Our Army connections pretty well confirmed it. They're also under enormous pressure. The SAS knows we've got people inside their system and they're taking the opportunity to cut them out. The least thing they need is to find out that they've got leaks that are benefitting your crew. Look, Bax, we lost two million pounds' worth of heroin on account of this caper, and we're losing more money every day on the street with all the police pressure. You've got to put an end to it."

"What do we do, just put her out on the street?"

"If you release her unharmed, she'll find out who you are and why you did what you did. We'll lose all of our political currency, Bax, everything. How do we convince the world we're fighting as loyal subjects of the Crown when we turn around and kidnap the Princess?"

"I'm not killing her, Eddie. What the hell do you think would happen if they found out we did that?"

"She needs to disappear so no one ever finds out, Bax. This is something you have to sort out on your own. Now, Doherty has a problem in Belfast he needs to settle. You'll probably read all about it in the papers. He'll be putting out his own fires, he doesn't need to tend to yours. We need you to resolve this by the middle of next week. Either he or Del will be coming out here to make sure you got the job done and take steps to bring you back in."

Cody said nothing to the rest of the team, living under the strain of having to terminate the mission over the next few days. The seven people in the barn had gone for over a week without bathing, which was proving almost traumatic to Jennifer. Cody finally sent Sammy and Vic out to a hardware store for a case of Sterno and metal gas cans. It allowed them to boil water without a campfire and let everyone take a whore's bath. He also made it a point to find the best take-out in Armagh and mix the orders so that large quantities were not purchased at any one place. He had them pick up a couple of board games as well to help everyone pass the time. It was far from perfect but made the wait time less stressful.

The team did not think much about the shooting on Lower Ormeau Road in Belfast. They thought it was just another sectarian attack. The mention of it happening next door to the place where the American Mercenaries had been attacked was something to consider. Cody figured that Ed Doherty was coming down hard against Republican sympathizers in the area, and only hoped there would be no repercussions. The last thing they needed was partisan activity inciting a search that could force them to leave the barn. Cody wasn't sure they could run much further. Sooner or later there would be a breaking point.

* * *

Ed Doherty's greatest concern was that Shannon Blackburn had not reached hers. He was well aware that the girl might have been mentally disturbed, but it had never been an issue until now. He had attempted to contact her numerous times after she failed to carry out the hit on the preacher to no avail. When he learned that she had defected, his worst fears were confirmed but he was unsure as to what to do. Having the preacher killed in a cowboy hit was intended to send a message to all of Belfast as well as Shannon Blackburn. Only her continued silence had to be resolved, and finally he sent a crew out to her home outside North Belfast. She agreed to meet him at the shipyards near downtown Belfast the next day.

"Shannon, believe me, I did not want to make that move without telling you ahead of time, but you left me no choice," the two walked along the dock as four gunmen watched from a distance. "You never let me down before. All of a sudden I find out you not only backed out on me, but switched sides on us. You could've at least given me a reason for what you've done."

"I've finally found what I wanted. I've found something for myself. What's done is done, you've put the fellow in hospital and he won't be out for a long time," Shannon said quietly. "I just want to be left alone, and your word that you'll leave him alone. The church is no threat to you, and it never will be. You've made your statement, now let us make peace."

"You put me in a bind, lass. I put a hit on the fellow in order to take the place out. Now you're asking me to leave it be."

"I've found a place of rest, Ed. I've found peace within myself. I won't surrender it to anyone. You've done what you felt you had to do. I've done everything you've ever asked me to do. I think we should both accept the church as a symbol of our friendship."

"Girl, you've got our people coming in and breaking bread with the Croppies. This is not good for business."

"Times are changing. People are not going to live divided by hatred forever. We're not calling people to come, they come of their own accord. Let it be, that's all I ask."

"All right, then," he conceded. He did not think it too much to ask in avoiding war against Shannon Blackburn. "Go your own way. If you ever change your mind, if you ever want to come back, you know where to find me."

Shannon walked him back to his car, and they hugged and kissed before the UDA men drove off. She headed back to her own parked vehicle, feeling a greater peace than she had ever known in her lifetime.

Deryl Lee Kilmarnoch's sacrifice had not been in vain.

Chapter Eight

Delmore Merrick, Eddie Mulvihill and Joe Emer walked into the abandoned warehouse in Armagh again, two hours after they had left. They had just suffered a traumatic experience in this very place and had no desire to have come back. Only the phone call that persuaded them was reason for the three older men, all in their sixties, to have turned their Volvo around and taken this long drive once again.

They drew their pistols though seeing no sight of any vehicles on the property. They knew there might be someone parked out back but did not want to drive into an ambush. They figured they would see if there was any sign of Baxter Cody or his men. If Cody was not here they would drive back into South Armagh and try to contact the Mid-Ulster Brigade in nearby Portadown. Ed Doherty had already been warned by the Inner Council not to seek help with the kidnapping, but the situation had changed drastically over the past few hours.

"Holy shite, Del," Eddie gasped as he stared in disbelief into the warehouse. "Will ye look at that!"

They stared in awe at the six bodies hanging upside down from the rafters wrapped in linen sheets. The trio could see the bodies twitching and rushed to the nearest one. Merrick produced a pocket knife and cut the linen from the face of the first man. They were astonished to see the features of Baxter Cody.

"They doped me up," Cody managed. "Cut me down."

"Geez, how in hell'd they get you up there?" Merrick looked furtively up at the metal beams overhead. "We'd have to crawl out onto those girders up there. We'd break our necks. Let me figure out something here."

"C'mon, Del, we just can't leave 'em up there," Mulvihill insisted.

"Get that pallet over there," Emer pointed to a far corner. "We'll hold it steady so one of us can climb up and cut the rope."

"What about the others?" Mulvihill watched as they wiggled and moaned at the sound of voices in the warehouse.

"What are we, squids? We can only do so much at a time. Let's get Bax down and he can help us."

The three men steadied the pallet on its side so that Emer, the tallest of them, could climb it as a ladder and shred the linen. Soon Cody's weight served to rip the cloth and send him tumbling down upon them. They lowered him to the ground and cut the ropes that bound his wrists and ankles.

"Geez, Bax, who the hell did this?" Merrick demanded.

"It was that terrorist Mansfield that Eddie told us about," Cody managed. "They fired gas grenades in here and took us out. They got the Princess."

"He got my number, he called me on my cell phone. He told us he took the Princess and that we needed to come back. I couldn't get you on your phone and knew something was up. Bax, we need to get backup. I'm going into Armagh and see if I can raise some fellows from the brigade at Portadown. We've got to at least have an alibi for what happened to Ed."

"The son of a bitch is toying with us. With the weapons they're carrying they could've nailed us at the cemetery at Londonderry. You guys go get us some backup, I'll get my guys down and get back to town. We can split our forces now the Princess is gone."

"All right, Bax, here's my knife," Merrick patted him on the back. "You look a bit under the weather. Be careful up there."

"I served with the Special Boat Service in Iraq," Cody grunted. "I won't have a problem. That's how I know how good Mansfield is. I never heard the bastards coming."

"We'll see how good he is when we put Bob Kerr's brigade up his arse," Merrick assured him. "Go on and get yer boys down, we'll settle this fellow's hash."

The three men left the warehouse and headed back to the Volvo. They climbed inside and gunned the engine, only when they began to take off they felt something dragging beneath the car.

"What in hell is that?" Joe Emer snarled, trying to back up though the vehicle seemed to get more entangled.

"Get out and take a look," Merrick ordered.

Emer dutifully exited the vehicle and squatted down, his face contorting into an expression of horror.

"Holy shit!" Emer cried out.

At once the car was illuminated by an overhead spotlight as a helicopter descended from the clouds above.

"This is a military transport! Get out of the car and lay face down on the ground! We will not hesitate to shoot! Get down on the ground now!"

The three UDA veterans knew the drill, getting down on their knees alongside the vehicle as they heard the roar of Army and police vehicles coming down the road from the north. Within minutes the property was crawling with RUC and UDR[1] soldiers who took both the three older men and the six volunteers inside the warehouse into custody.

The nightmare started for Delmore Merrick when he and Ed Doherty, along with Mulvihill and Emer, arrived at the warehouse hours ago. They had directed the kidnap team to the property at the behest of the Mid-Ulster Brigade after the Inner Council had made it clear to Doherty that they would have nothing to do with the operation. They would help as best they could but would make no direct contact with the kidnappers. Doherty agreed, letting them know he was arriving in Armagh to resolve the issue once and for all.

Doherty nearly lit into him when he entered the warehouse and was given a military salute by Cody. He had all he could stand of this Army stuff but would deal with it at the proper time.

"Okay, lad, where's the girl?" he asked.

"Upstairs. We've got her tied to a bed we found in an office on the second level."

"All well and good. I think Del's made it clear what our situation is in this matter," he stared at Cody. The four men were dressed in suits and ties, wearing overcoats and fedoras in the nippy spring weather. "Right now no one's sure as to who took her, but all hell will come down if they ever find out. We're still trying to blame it on the Croppies, and that's who the Army and MI6 are looking at. There's rumors those Americans you saw at the Crown Bar are still in the game, but that's neither here nor there. Now, you know about them wasting Murphy and Bernard, and you know Mc Lintock got taken down along with my heroin shipment. The RUC came in right behind those Evil Mother

---

1. Ulster Defense Regiment

bastards, and Mc Lintock's entire crew's on ice at Maghaberry Prison. That's fourteen men and two million pounds of merchandise I've lost. This problem has to be solved tonight, Bax. There's no other way around it."

"I'm open to suggestions, sir."

"Let's go on up there," Doherty nodded at the metal stairs leading to the cat-walk on the upper level. Cody led the way as Doherty and Merrick followed him up the steps. Sammy, Emer and Mulvihill lit cigarettes as they waited down-stairs together.

Jennifer was handcuffed to a metal cot in a small office space. Her hair was tangled into a bun and her black sweatsuit needed washing. Her heart was racing as she heard the voices downstairs, and she sensed something important was happening. This was the first time anyone from their organization had come out to meet with them. After all this time, she suspected that some important decision had been made. They had been driving around the country for over two weeks and nearly got captured twice. She heard aircraft and emergency sirens countless times throughout her ordeal, but to no avail. She could only pray now that their demands had been met and a deal had been arranged with the abductors to set her free.

The door was opened and she watched apprehensively as the two elderly men came into the room followed by Cody. The white-haired man came around and stared down at her as if inspecting a slab of beef.

"Well, this is it, then," Doherty said gruffly. "Do what you have to."

"What?" Cody squinted at him.

"Aren't—aren't you gonna let me go?" Jennifer insisted. "You can't tell me they haven't made concessions after all this time. Surely someone's agreed to something by now. Who have you been talking to?"

"Ed," Delmore said plaintively, realizing this was not going to go down well at all.

"Sir, permission to discuss this in private," Cody demanded.

"Son, I don't know what ye thought was going to happen here, but I told ye it was all over," Doherty pulled back his coat and drew a .38 from his shoulder holster. "Ye can step outside if ye like."

"Wait, hold on, guys," tears welled in Jennifer's eyes as she pulled against her handcuff. "I don't know who you talked to or what this is about, but there's nothing you'll gain by doing this. I have no power or authority, getting rid of me isn't going to resolve anything. I know someone somewhere would pay you a reasonable amount to let me go if you asked. Killing me won't do accomplish anything. C'mon, fellows, I don't want to die."

"This is not going to happen, Ed," Cody pulled his Glock from his waistband and pointed it at Doherty's head. "Put that weapon away or I pull the trigger."

"Are you outta yer feckin' mind, Baxter?" Doherty stared in disbelief.

"Bax, put that thing away!" Merrick stared in astonishment.

"I'm not gonna ask you again," Cody warned him. "Put the gun away now!"

Cody watched the hammer of the revolver move a fraction before pulling the trigger. The Glock went off like a bomb as Ed Doherty's head exploded like a gourd, his brain matter spurting across the wall behind him. Delmore Merrick reeled back in shock as Jennifer buried her face in the mattress, stifling a cry of horror.

"Okay, Del, you're in charge," Cody pointed the pistol at his head.

"What?" Merrick gasped. "What are you talking about?"

"It's your call. Either I stand behind you or against you. What's it gonna be?"

"All right," he managed. "Okay, I can clean this up. I'll tell the guys downstairs Ed pulled a gun on you and you had no choice. It's over now, Bax, put that thing away. Please."

"I'll take him with us and we'll dump him somewhere. You make up a story and I'll back you up on it. You decide what we're gonna do here. Either you ask for a ransom or I'm letting her go. This has gone on long enough. I suggest you make some kind of statement before we let her go so that the whole operation hasn't been in vain."

"I'll speak up for you, I swear," Jennifer sobbed. "Whatever you want to say I'll say it, and I'll stand up for you. No matter whose side you're on, I agree that the Troubles have gone on too long. I'll insist there be no retribution of any kind. Just let me go back and do what I can to bring this to an end."

"I'll take her to another room," Cody told Del. "You send Sammy and another of my guys up here. I'm sure they heard the gunshot and they'll come in. You go back to Belfast and tell everyone about the change of command. Let everybody know we'll be back to stand behind you in whatever you decide to do."

"I'll contact you as soon as I reach Belfast. Just hold tight and lay low, you'll hear from me in a couple of hours at most."

Merrick told his partners what happened, and they were stunned by the development but had no choice but to back Delmore's play and see what happened next.

"So the four of you arrived and Cody and his men were nowhere to be found. You searched the property and the three of you got separated from Ed Doherty. You started back to Belfast for reinforcements and got the anonymous call. You drove back and found Baxter Cody and his men hanging like slabs of beef from the ceiling. You cut Cody loose, went back on your way, but found Ed Doherty's body under your car."

"Mark, I'm sixty-six years old, I just found my best friend's body under my motorcar after cutting one of those boys loose from hanging from the rafters in there," Delmore Merrick ran his fingers through his hair. They had been taken to RUC Headquarters in Armagh and were grilled separately by Mark O'Shaughnessy as well as different RUC and UDR officers at the facility. "I'm trying to remember things as best I can."

"I don't even have to compare notes with any of the other fellows to see your story's gonna leak like a rusty bucket," Mark shook his head as he sat across the metal table from Merrick in the small room. "You know, this isn't a regular kidnapping. This is being seen as a terror attack against the British Empire. We can talk terms with kidnappers but we don't deal with terrorists. Any way this goes down, you and your old friends are going away for the rest of your natural lives, and your new friends won't get out until they're as old as you are now."

"Help me, Mark," Merrick pleaded. "Help me out of this mess."

"We both have to pin this whole affair on Berlin Mansfield," Mark explained patiently. "It's going to be a lot easier for me to wrap this up with no mess. I know about Kevin Moore giving Cody up to Mansfield, but that's already classified and I can make it stay that way. If we make it look like Doherty authorized Cody and his men to hunt down Mansfield, Eddie the Bull dies a hero and you and Cody are off the hook. Now, if that girl comes in and testifies that Cody was the one who snatched her at the Crown Bar, all bets are off. I think you and your boys had better pray that she becomes a casualty of the rescue operation."

"Could you do that for me, Mark?" the old man begged.

"That I cannot do," Mark turned to leave. "I'll see to it that your solicitors get to meet with all of you, and that you have time to get your stories straight. Other than that, you'd better hope that Mansfield finishes the job that you people have totally mucked up."

* * *

Baxter Cody remembered hearing the soft crunch of gravel outside and thought it was either Sammy and Vic taking Doherty's body away, or Merrick and his lieutenants returning for whatever reason. The tires had rolled in too leisurely to have been anyone else. Even if it was one cop car or a lost motorist getting his bearings, it wasn't anything they couldn't handle after all this.

"Omigosh, did you hear that!" Jennifer gasped. He had been trying to calm her down after watching Doherty's head getting nearly blown off. He felt as if he had succeeded somewhat, and a lot of it had to do with the fact that she knew Cody had saved her life.

"Don't worry, I'll go check it out. Are you gonna be okay?"

"I'd be a lot better if you took this handcuff off."

"I told you, I can't risk the lives of any of my men. I think we've had enough death for one night. This area's got to be crawling with cops, and if they come in here in force, more people will die. I know I don't want that and neither do you."

"I know how close we are to ending this now. I'm not going to do anything stupid, you've got to realize that."

"Jennifer, you've got to trust me just a little while longer. You're right, it's almost over."

"Black SUV outside," Joe Coolio held his Uzi at the ready as he and the others crouched at the windows on the east side overlooking the gravel driveway. "The driver got out, he's holding a map up to the light. I can't see anyone else in the vehicle."

"Sammy, Vic, you two check out the other side of the building. He might have let someone out on the road before he rolled in here."

"Gotcha."

Everything was a blur after that. He remembered moving carefully out behind Sammy and Vic to make sure they weren't waylaid. He saw them slip into the darkness and it got too quiet after that. Cody flipped the safety on his Uzi and moved forward, and after that he must have gotten hit with a tranquilizer dart in the neck. He tried to get back inside and warn the others but it was like getting hit with a heavyweight right cross. He slipped and fell like a stone drunk and could feel hands grabbing him, dragging him, relieving him of his weapon. His wrists and ankles were tied and they left him on the concrete before the fireworks went off.

"So your story works well for everyone. You and your men went in and checked out this abandoned warehouse on a hunch, and the kidnappers waylaid you. Delmore Merrick was scheduled to meet you and wound up rescuing the lot of you after finding you hanging from the ceiling like a bunch of tampons."

Mark O'Shaughnessy waited until Jon and Slash arrived before going in to see Baxter Cody, who was just starting to come around from the tranquilizer dart and a shot of morphine administered by the Mansfield Gang. Baxter was surly and seemed intent to show his captors that he was a stand-up guy who would not roll over or be intimidated. Jon and Slash felt like Mark was comfortably settling in behind the driver's seat at this point, and it could start getting ugly.

"Just doing my duty for God and Country, and not getting paid for it, I might add."

"It looks like you find plenty of ways to make your money. Fringe benefits, hm?" Mark looked at his hand-held PC tablet. "Smuggling, racketeering, drug trafficking, extortion, assault, and now kidnapping. I might ask what God and what country you're referring to."

"Those are all trumped-up charges that the military and its police flunkies railroaded me on, and not very well, considering the time I served."

"You've had a lot of breaks, but not this time. First we'll keep you in solitary and spread the word that you've squealed like a pig on everyone you know. After that we'll break Kevin Moore's crew and exchange time for their word that they aided and abetted you with the Princess kidnapping. By the time I'm through, they'll put you away for a thousand years."

"Everyone on Newtownards Road knows I'm dead on solid. They know I'd never roll over, especially for a prick like you."

With that Mark smashed him across the jaw with a crushing right, sending Cody crashing to the floor from his metal chair. Jon and Slash got up and pulled him up by each arm.

"Listen, you little bastard, I'll have you killed in prison if you don't get with the program," Mark motioned for the CIA agents to set him back in his chair. He produced a manila envelope and spread a dozen photos across the table before him. "This is the man who killed Kevin Moore, attacked you in Port Muck and Londonderry, and hung you like a slab of beef here in Armagh. He's the one you saw the Princess with."

"His name is Berlin Mansfield. All the newspapers have is his yearbook pictures from the University of Berlin. These are current but unfortunately none match. Do you recognize any of them?"

"Sure."

"Which one?"

"Whichever one you like."

"Listen, asshole, if me and my friend here decide to take a birdwalk, they'll be carrying you out on a stretcher by the time we get back," Jon leaned over from behind Cody. "Just give him the right answers and we'll get you out of here."

"What do you mean, get me out?"

"Someone has to go back to East Belfast and restore the balance of power now that Ed Doherty's gone. If we let you go and spread the word we found Doherty with his head blown off, wedged under Merrick's Volvo, people just might believe it. That'll leave you to make sure Merrick's able to keep whatever's left on the table. You bastards are cleared of the kidnapping, the UDA retains its prestige and political currency, and I—and my associates here—get to rescue the Princess."

"Whatever you say," Cody wiped the blood from his nose and mouth.

"Your signed confession," Mark pulled a printed statement from the folder and set it down on the table with a pen alongside it. "We'll have you back on Newtownards Road in forty-eight hours. If we let you and Merrick and friends out any sooner, the rest of your gang will know something's not right."

"Yeah, sure," Cody scribbled on the papers.

"One more thing. Your eye. Stand up," Mark requested. Cody put down the pen and stood up. Mark hauled off and hit him with a thunderous right cross that hurtled him into the corner where he collapsed in a heap.

"Hmm," Mark grunted in pain as he flexed his fist, the agents staring at him in apprehension. "Well, now you look like you've been questioned. A word to the wise: don't ever do anything that stupid again, at least not without checking with us."

Jon and Slash looked down at Cody, whose eyebrow was torn open and his eye quickly puffing into a purple mass. They remained speechless as they followed Mark out of the small interview room.

* * *

Jennifer had been lying on the cot in the warehouse, having turned her back on the gore-splattered wall where Ed Doherty's brains remained caked on the sheetrock. She listened desperately to the sounds downstairs and could hear the doors opening and closing though it grew more and more quiet. She knew the British Army was one of the best in the world and the SAS was second to none, though most of what she knew of their abilities was from TV and the movies. She knew if they arrived her tribulation would be over. Only whoever was outside was not moving as quickly or decisively as she would have liked.

After nearly a half hour passed as an eternity, she could hear voices screaming 'Gas!' and scrambling about downstairs. She heard a lot of crashing and yelling before things grew quiet again. There were strange voices now, and she grew very afraid as she could not hear the voices of Cody's team any longer.

At once the door flew open and the light was switched on, and Jennifer recoiled to the end of her cot before staring in astonishment as the figure standing before her.

"Jim!" she cried out. "Jim Jones! Omigosh! I can't believe it!"

"Princess," he smiled, a black balaclava pulled back from his face, clad in a black combat uniform. "Thank goodness you are okay. Pull your wrist away from the bedpost."

Jennifer did so, and Berlin Mansfield swung a machete with all his might, hacking the links asunder so she was freed. She jumped up and threw herself sobbing into his arms.

"Hey, Boss, it's all clear," Kurt the Bruiser appeared in the doorway, dressed similarly to Mansfield as they all were. He saw the Princess cradled in Berlin's arms and gave him a big grin.

"Good. Proceed with the plan. Have Chopper meet me at the truck so we can remove the Princess' bracelet. Tell the team they have ten mikes[2]."

"Roger that," Kurt raced down the catwalk. Mansfield took her hand and led her down the steps into the shadowy darkness that encompassed the warehouse. The only light came in through the large industrial windows from the moon above. Cody's men, and now Mansfield's, used flashlights unless they could switch on lights in windowless rooms that could not be seen from outside. Chuck Chop came outside behind them and retrieved a heavy set of bolt cutters to cut Jennifer's cuff loose.

"Oh, my gosh," she rubbed her wrist, trying to get her thoughts in order. "I can't believe it. I'm so hungry, and I need a shower so bad. Are you taking me straight to the police station? Is there any place I can go first to get sorted out?"

---

2. minutes

"Actually, I wanted to explain the situation to you in detail," he turned to her as Chuck went back to rejoin his comrades in stringing up Cody and his men, unknown to Jennifer. "This whole thing has been part of a large conspiracy. The men who kidnapped you were part of the Ulster Defense Association, Northern Ireland's largest Loyalist organization. Throughout your ordeal, the connection between the kidnappers and the UDA has been covered up by the government. They have never even made a ransom demand or given a reason as to the kidnapping. Obviously it was done in an effort to end the peace talks. Princess, I would want to know I am delivering you into safe hands before I brought you in, do you understand?"

"Yes—yes, of course," Jennifer managed, trying to absorb what he told her. "But—who was it who tried to rescue me at the farmhouse, and the last warehouse?"

"That was us, me and my friends."

"Who—who are you working for?"

"I'm a volunteer with the Republicans. I have no ties with the IRA. I took this mission on my own accord. I held no rank with Sinn Fein when I met you at the dance before you were kidnapped. I just wanted to be part of the peace process, it was a personal matter. When you were taken, I took it upon myself to rescue you. I want to see peace in Northern Ireland, and I know you are the answer. This is why I want to be sure that you are returned safely, and not back into the hands of the conspirators."

"But who are you? Are you some kind of secret agent?"

"I'm what you might call a soldier of fortune. I have fought in the Serbian War and in Africa. My father is a native Irishman and it has always been my dream to see peace in Northern Ireland. I was born and raised in Germany and I know what it is like to live in a divided country. I believe that fate brought me to the conference and allowed me to intervene when you were abducted. My only wish now is your safe return so you can finish what you started."

"Okay, Boss, we're ready to go," Kurt joined them along with the others back at the SUV.

"Good. Let's get back to the safe house and get ourselves situated."

They drove towards Lough Ross along Highway A37 going west through Newry, where they stopped at a farmhouse not far from the lake. Mansfield had implored Mike O'Beirne to intercede with the Provisional IRA's South Armagh Brigade, and they were given access to the property along with pre-delivered supplies. Mansfield ordered the team to secure the perimeter and set up positions on the bottom floor, while he and Jennifer took the upper floor. She immediately drew herself a hot bath while Mansfield got on the phone with O'Beirne.

"Everything is secure on my end. I believe it is time to put the next phase of the operation into effect."

"Dammit, Berlin," Mike was aggravated. "I keep telling you not to call here and you keep telling me about your secure line feeds, yet people are being hauled in by the government every single day. You won't talk to any of my associates, and now you're wanting to aggravate the situation despite the fact you've already completed the rescue mission."

"If I send her back now, it turns into a Loyalist victory. They've set the peace talks back for the better part of a month and will have convinced the world that it was an IRA plot regardless of what she says. The government will concede that no harm has been done and will pretend it never happened. It will become a freak accident, a sidenote in the annals of history. If we let the military play into our hands, she will go back to the table with greater resolve than ever. Trust me on this, Michael. Just put the South Armagh Brigade on alert and I'll handle the rest."

"I'll contact Tom Murphy and see what he wants to do. Don't call here again."

Mansfield went back upstairs and waited until Jennifer finished showering, and took his turn in the bathroom as she prepared for bed. He removed his wig and makeup, taking a shower, shaving and brushing his teeth before retiring. He pulled on the sweat pants he brought along with him and headed back into the room, almost running right into Jennifer as she went back in for another towel.

Historians would long speculate as to what created the phenomenon. Many would compare it to the Patty Hearst syndrome, as the captive is brainwashed and develops a bond with her captors in believing they are united in their flight from their pursuers. Others would point to her deprivation and emotional need for security resulting in a breakdown of her resistance. There were others who would say that she might have been hypnotized by the high-tech terror gang.

Jennifer was caught entirely off-guard by Mansfield, stripped naked to the waist. She had not been with a man since her husband died, and was taken aback by this man with whom she felt a physical attraction from their first meeting.

"You—you've changed," she looked up at him, loosening the grip on her terrycloth robe. "You—you're different somehow."

"You," he said softly, gazing into her emerald eyes. "You're beautiful."

"No," she reached up and touched his face. "You."

It was as if an irresistible attraction had come between them, drawing their lips inexorably together. They kissed softly, then desperately, hungry for one another. The robe dropped from her shoulders and he felt her bare breasts against his chest. He lifted her in his arms and carried her to one of the single beds on the opposite sides of the room, gently lowering her and kneeling beside her. She put her arms around his neck and continued kissing him as he climbed onto the bed with her. He penetrated her and she gasped with pleasure, wrapping her legs around him as they entwined with passion. They fell into a vortex of splendor until after a long, long time, they exhausted each other and fell into a blissful sleep.

They woke up at dawn to the smell of coffee and fried food wafting from downstairs. They both awakened with a start, tensing as they came to consciousness in each other's arms. Mansfield was used to being in situations where he had to fight for his life in a moment's notice. Jennifer had been under the stress of a lifetime over the past couple of weeks and was jolted by the effect of having a pair of loving arms around her.

"It's okay," he stroked her cheek, shifting his weight to give her some space on the small mattress. "You're safe."

Her eyes searched his face, still trying to remember whether this was all a dream. She reached up and touched his cheek, realizing that this was her dream lover that she fell asleep with.

"What happens now?" she asked softly.

"I'm making arrangements to bring you to British and American agents by sundown," he replied. "This way there's no chance of a double-cross. We'll have the area secure and we'll be on open ground. If something does go wrong, we'll have no problem getting you back out."

"My gosh, I can't believe this," she turned and stared up at the ceiling. "This is a nightmare. My own people. How could such a thing be happening?"

"This is what you must bring back with you, my dear," he sat up on the edge of the bed. "You must return with all this information to make sure it never happens again."

"We'd better get dressed," she sat up.

"There's a brand new sweat suit on the chair by the other bed," he pointed as he rose and put his own sweat suit and track shoes on. "Socks, underwear—I figured you were a medium."

"Thanks," she blushed. "You knew you were gonna rescue me, didn't you?"

"Yes, I did."

"You hadn't—planned on—sleeping with me, did you?"

"A man can dream, can't he?" he smiled softly before going downstairs to rejoin the others.

Sting Ramapril was a gourmet chef who specialized in West Indian cuisine, and had made rodent meat taste like a restaurant entrée when they were hiding out in the jungles of Africa. Here with the resources supplied by the IRA's South Armagh Brigade, he came up with a breakfast of tarragon omelets, steak strips and buttered soda bread that left everyone stuffed and satisfied. Jennifer was introduced to the team and found them as personable as Cody's gang. She was growing more and more enthralled by Jim Jones and wondered what the future might hold for them.

"Say, Berl—uh, Jim," Benny Van Tran as they went about their assignments, "what were you planning on doing between now and sunset? We've got a bunch of time on our hands."

"Well, there's a very nice lake up the road," Mansfield replied. "Perhaps we can take turns riding up there. If we split the group I doubt we'll attract undue suspicion."

The team looked at one another in amazement.

"Of course," Al the Cat grinned. "Nobody would expect a couple of guys walking around with the Princess of Edinburgh at a lake in broad daylight."

"Precisely."

"I think I'm gonna sit around here and watch some TV," Chuck announced. "We've got a couple of cases of beer in the fridge, so I'll just chill out here. If I see any helicopter sorties or hear any explosions out by the lake, I'll go on and call a cab back to Belfast."

Eventually the rest of the team agreed, and so it was that Mansfield and Jennifer took the Citroen SUV up to the lake while the others relaxed at the farmhouse. They both wore ski caps and sunglasses, and looked no different than any other couple enjoying the lovely day. Jennifer found this to be a day unlike any other she could remember since her husband died. She had not dated or otherwise been with a male companion, and had done very little outside of the public eye away from Royal security forces. She held his arm as they walked along the road surrounding the lake and held hands as they made their way down to the fishing docks. Sometimes she had to remind herself that this was not just a vacation, and that she had watched a man's head blown out less than twenty-four hours ago.

They returned around 4 PM as Sting had prepared a steak and lobster dinner with curry rice and an excellent Merlot. Jennifer and the team enjoyed the meal and exchanged banter as Kurt took a ride into town to make sure everything was set for the scheduled trip in a couple of hours. By now she was girding herself for her return to Buckingham Palace and the endless interviews ahead. She only hoped Jim would remain beside her and continue to give her strength.

He proved to be an excellent conversationalist and did not once speak of politics, her tribulation or the grueling tasks awaiting her. They spoke of their travels throughout Europe and their mutual love of art and music. She told him all about her childhood in Scotland, and he told her about his days at the University. She felt as if she had known him for years when they returned, and she only hoped that they could build on this incident as something for the future.

Kurt the Bruiser drove out to the Newtownhamilton district, well-known for its Cattle Mart as well as being a low-income community. He set up a seventy-pound bomb in a vacant building thirty yards from a housing complex, waiting until there was no sign of pedestrian activity before setting it off. He immediately called the police and waited until they arrived before driving off. He then called ahead to Mansfield and reported the mission had been completed.

A convoy from the British Army was dispatched from the barracks at Crossmaglen, reinforced by a platoon of UDR soldiers. The RUC also turned out in force, setting up checkpoints and roadblocks around the predominantly Catholic neighborhood in response to what they perceived as an IRA bombing. The logic was that the building had been used by the UDA as a staging area for some of their own operations, and had been demolished as a warning to the loyalist community.

This set off an alert throughout the Republican neighborhoods of South Armagh, who were also preparing for an onslaught by British and loyalist forces. The IRA's regional brigade began mobilizing at once, with every available man reporting to his unit and heading to Newtownhamilton. The volunteers began taking strategic positions along the outskirts of the neighborhood as police and military vehicles began rolling down the main thoroughfares.

The residents heard the sound of emergency vehicles arriving, and women and children sent out the alarm in the traditional manner of banging trashcan lids and cooking pots in doorways and windows. It was the signal for all able-bodied men to rise in defense of the community. Some men brought out pistols and hunting rifles, while others brought flammable liquids and gathered bottles and rags for Molotov cocktails. Children also collected sticks and stones for the battle ahead, while women produced first-aid kits and medical supplies.

As police cars began driving down the streets of Newtownhamilton, they kept running up against hastily-contrived roadblocks made of garbage cans, used tires and bundles of trash. The officers got out of the vehicles to move the barriers and were pelted by rocks and bottles from the rooftops and behind parked cars. They started to draw their weapons but saw children and teenagers running from their hiding spots. They next radioed for backup, and police trucks began moving in behind them. Officers in riot gear began to deploy, making room for detainees in the twelve-man paddy wagons. Army units were also informed as to a potential riot in the making.

Once the trucks arrived, volunteers on the rooftops began tossing the Molotov cocktails down. Many of the trucks exploded into flames, causing the police to take up firing positions around corners and in doorways. They, in turn, were pelted by sticks and stones thrown by the youths, causing the riot squad to deploy. They began fastening fire hoses to nearby hydrants and passing out rubber bullets. They alerted the UDR units of the situation, causing them to bring their vehicles up to support the police units.

The regular Army troops sent in the bomb squad to buildings adjacent to the explosion site and found themselves under a volley of rifle fire. They took cover and soon detected snipers occupying positions along the rooftops of tenements along the outskirts of the residential area. They summoned their armored cars, which rolled towards the buildings and provided mobile cover for troops returning fire and surrounding the tenements. Only the snipers were far deadlier than their civilian counterparts and wounded a number of soldiers unused to urban warfare. Most of the problems facing the soldiers was refraining from shooting residents watching from windows.

Eventually one of the British Army regulars spotted one of the positions in a top floor apartment window and directed machine gun fire at the sniper nest.

There was a secondary explosion inside the building and the squad reported that the enemy had been taken out. Only minutes later, a white flag appeared from the side windows of the top floor. Residents began yelling that an old man had been killed and a woman seriously injured by the explosion. The soldiers warned them to evacuate the building but once again were forced to take cover under rifle fire.

Mansfield and his crew entered the SUV as soon as the Bruiser got word that the resistance was underway. Jennifer had no idea of what was going on as Sting had insisted on watching the conclusion of the soccer match between England and Jamaica. They all got dressed and the gang quietly loaded the Citroen with equipment before they headed out to Newtownhamilton. Kurt had gotten on the Internet and found the best roads to taking in avoiding the police barricades. He gave Al the Cat the directions, and shortly they were on their way.

They could hear the sounds of screaming and automatic fire within blocks of the residential area, and Al slowed the truck as they cruised down one of the side streets. They could see smoke and flames along the pavement as women and children wept in flight from the police.

"My goodness, what's happening?" Jennifer stared out the side window on the passenger side. "It looks like some kind of disturbance."

"Your people are under attack," Mansfield replied as he sat beside her. "Al, pull up close so we can get out and take a look."

They got out of the vehicle and watched as the police began firing rubber bullets into a crowd pressing towards the intersection. Women and children began screaming, and they saw one teenager fall to the sidewalk clutching her eye.

"You see how they attack your people, Princess?" Mansfield pointed angrily at the altercation. "They are shooting rubber bullets at innocent civilians!"

"No!" she cried, running up the street. "I won't allow it!"

"Get your weapons ready," Mansfield ordered Kurt before taking off after her.

"Stop what you're doing right now!" Jennifer screamed as she confronted two of the UDR troopers manning the hose at the fire hydrant.

"What the—!" the men stared at her, suddenly very aware of who she looked like. "Get off the street, missus, there's a riot in progress!"

"You stop it right now!" she demanded. "I am your Princess!"

"Listen, madam, you'd better get on about your business or we'll have you arrested!"

"Don't you tell me what to do, I'll have you fired!"

"All right," the soldier waved to a group of policemen waiting to force the crowd back after the volley of rubber bullets was fired. "C'mon, come get this one here!"

"You may have bitten off more than you can chew this time," Mansfield admonished them. "Come on, dear, we can catch the rest of this on the telly."

He pulled her away despite her objections as Kurt and the others drew closer, holding their RPG-7's behind their backs.

"Wait until I get her in the truck," he told Kurt as they passed. He took Jennifer's hand and walked her back to the Citroen, taking her in his arms after he opened the back door.

"This is terrible, just terrible," she wept. "How are we going to stop this?"

"When you return to the Palace and report all you've seen," he insisted. "Come on, we'll go back to the farmhouse and try it again tomorrow after things settle down."

Mansfield looked out the window and gave Kurt a nod just as the police rushed down the street in search of the Princess look-alike and her friend. They were greatly concerned that such an imitator could cause an even greater furor among the civilians. As they approached the parked vehicle, they saw that the couple had given way to men carrying rocket launchers.

They began yelling and darting for cover, but the gas grenades sailed into their midst and exploded against the pavement. They released a black gas that paralyzed their faces, filling their facial orifices with pus and mucus. The officers tried spitting the mucus out but it expanded with a jelly-like consistency, nearly choking them to death. They fell to the ground, doing their best to cough enough mucus out to catch a single breath.

"Kinda choked them out there, Boss," Kurt grinned as they tossed the weapons into the hatch, climbing into the Citroen and driving back to the farmhouse.

Mark O'Shaughnessy arrived a half hour later, learning that Mansfield's gas grenades had seriously incapacitated six RUC officers. He decided to inform the press at last that the Golden Terror was at large in Ulster, and was the prime suspect in the kidnapping of the Princess of Edinburgh.

Chapter Nine

A Place to Pray had begun focusing its efforts on the Princess Search, which served well to ameliorate tensions between Shannon Blackburn and the new Belfast UDA godfather, Delmore Merrick. The new boss was in a benevolent mood after having been released from custody and was reserved though receptive to her overtures. She asked for a sizable donation in expanding the Church facility to provide for the new mission and he reluctantly complied. Although the Church remained open for prayer, they had no one to replace Deryl at the pulpit. Shannon considered that in changing the Church's grand strategy.

The Church continued to draw visitors from both neighborhoods, and the loyalist community could not censure the effort lest it be seen as conspiring to derail the peace talks. The UDA Inner Council issued a general order that no one was to do anything to be seen as hindering the rescue effort. This provided for a seamless transition as Shannon began putting up posters and distributing flyers in rallying the people to take a hand in searching for Jennifer.

There had been so many donations after Deryl was shot that Shannon was able to heavily invest in promotional materials that turned over a quick profit. It facilitated her plan to drive out to Armagh to take an active role in the Princess Search in the vicinity. She knew that a high-profile appearance would do wonders in alleviating tensions within the community, accrediting the ministry in a key contribution to the peace process in Armagh.

Everyone who met Shannon, including Jon and Slash, were highly impressed by her intelligence and cunning. They did some checking after Deryl was shot to see who would be handling his affairs while he remained in hospital. They found she had a lengthy record with the RUC, the entirely of which was classified. That normally indicated a supergrass, so they let it go at that. They met her once at the hospital and stopped by to visit at the Church. They were stricken by her beauty as was everyone who met her, but her smooth manner and absolute confidence were qualities they had seen in few men in their travels.

Deryl's condition improved from critical to stable after a time. His ribcage was entirely shattered by the shotgun blasts but miraculously his heart and lungs survived the barrage. He continued to pray from his hospital bed and was receiving visitors throughout the day who provided encouragement, cards and gifts. Shannon eventually had to recruit from the congregation to have people bring the dozens of flowers from the hospital to the Church. He had entrusted her with the operation of the Church and was in full accord with her desire to devote its efforts to the Princess Search as a gambit to unite the people of the Belfast community and all of Ulster.

And so it was that she arrived at sunrise following the riot in Newtownhamilton along with a rented eighteen-wheeler and a dozen volunteers. They parked as close as possible to the site of the bombed warehouse near Cattle Mart and quickly reached out to the ranchers and cattle traders in the area. They knew that a Princess Search event would be a boon for business and gladly offered to help in any way they could. Having such a beautiful woman in charge certainly did not hurt matters. They watched approvingly as the group began unloading promotional materials and tables which they set up alongside the truck.

On this Sunday morning, families preparing for Mass saw the displays and began coming over to see what was going on. Children began running back to their apartments to pester their parents for money to buy Princess coozies, T-shirts and other souvenirs. This caused their older siblings to come out to chat with the volunteers, especially Shannon. It was not long before their parents came out, promising to stop by after the local church services were over.

Shannon was well-prepared for the opportunity, bringing along a couple of barbecue grills and cooking pots. They also bought a few heads of cabbage with which to make stew. The cattle traders caught on and sent for some sausage links to attract customers. People from the Protestant community heard what was going on and came out to inquire. Soon there was a gathering as diverse as any that had assembled at the storefront in Belfast. It promised to be an interesting day ahead.

At the farmhouse outside Newry, the team was not expecting much activity until nightfall. Mansfield contacted Mike O'Beirne and this time was given a direct contact number to a representative of the South Armagh Brigade. The plan was for the gang to bring the Princess through Crossmaglen en route to Dundalk. From there they would be able to cross the Irish Sea by boat to the Isle of Man. There they could make arrangements for the Princess to return to London. Mansfield was now concerned with running into an Army ambush that could get Jennifer killed. He suspected he might have flexed too much muscle the night before and was now second-guessing any further aggression against the Brits, though it was a great temptation.

His worst distraction beside Jennifer was the opportunity to continue outwitting the Brits on the field. He knew the reputation of the SAS and was savoring the taste of victory after three encounters. Had he been able to command troops on the field during this conflict, he felt as if he could have ended it in a very short time. This was an insurgent war like no other. It was a rebel force enjoying public and international support, consisting of seasoned and dedicated volunteers who had gotten their experience fighting the SAS. Yet they considered themselves patriots and loathed the thought of being seen in the same light as the Mansfield Gang.

"Well, here's the supplies from town," Al announced as he and Benny returned from their early morning drive. "Did you want to run recon on that road and make sure we've got no surprises ahead tonight?"

"I suppose so," Mansfield replied as he pulled on his running jacket. "I think they're probably nursing their bloody noses from last night."

"I don't know how those Brits got the reps they have," Kurt shrugged as he pulled the thick newspaper apart. "You know, you could just sell the IRA a case of those gas canisters and the Brits'd be suing for peace a lot quicker."

"Hey, they're playing with kid gloves," Sting pointed out. "If this was Serbia or Africa, they would've blown that neighborhood to kingdom come for the shit they pulled."

"Kid gloves?" Chuck squinted at him. "Rubber bullets and water hoses?"

"I'd take a water hosing over a shell from a tank barrel any day," Sting grunted. "I'm making breakfast, so Berlin, you better hurry back."

"See, it's like I told you," Chuck teased, pointing at Sting. "*He's* the Evil Mother."

"Where's the Princess?" Benny asked.

"Upstairs catching up on her beauty sleep," Mansfield replied. "I think last night went past her limit. If she comes down, tell her I'll be back shortly. If she wants to go outside, give her a hat and shades and make sure someone goes with her."

"Aye aye, Captain Kirk," Kurt grunted, busying himself with the sports pages.

Jennifer heard the voices downstairs, yawning and stretching as she prepared for what she hoped would mark her return to London. The grim reality of what happened last night sobered her, and she climbed out of bed and headed for the bathroom. She saw Berlin had risen early and gave him brownie points for not getting some while she was sleeping. She knew he was probably downstairs planning their next move, and she had no reason not to trust him entirely.

What she had witnessed changed her entire perspective on the Troubles. She had done a vast amount of research on the conflict and was well familiar with the horror stories. The difference was seeing it in person, watching the police firing rubber bullets and hosing down people just outside their own homes. She had no doubt that there was provocation. What had to happen was for the hostilities to end, once and for all. Even in the most primitive societies, when two people fought you didn't wait and asked who started it. You stepped in to break it up. She would never forget the sight of the teenage girl holding her eye after getting hit with the rubber bullet than she would forget what happened to Ed Doherty.

She took a shower and dressed in her sweatsuit again, thankful she had a fresh change of underwear though she did put her things from yesterday to soak. She set them out to dry and made her way downstairs, the smell of fried food making her tummy growl.

"Hey, the Princess!" Chuck announced, and they all got a chuckle over the singsong chorus of 'Good morning, Princess' sounding like grade schoolers.

"Good morning men, at ease," she giggled.

"We've got coffee and buttered bread," Sting looked out from the kitchen. "Berlin's scouting the road, he'll be back in a few minutes."

"Who?" she asked.

"That's our nickname for him. They call me Brooklyn half the time," Kurt stared at Sting.

"I'll take coffee," she replied. "Ooh, can I see the paper?"

"Sure," Kurt nodded. "You can take it upstairs if you want. These guys don't have much language discipline in the morning, if you know what I mean."

"Okay," she said, grabbing the tabloid insert along with the ads and the comics. She knew that it would make it easier for them to relax without a woman around as well. She thanked Sting for a cup of coffee and headed back upstairs.

She set the cup down on the small table by the window and idly flipped through the parts of the paper she figured no one wanted. She saw her picture on the front page of the tabloid and refused to read the story. All it would do was upset her more than she was already. She did not even like to read the tabloids when she was up and around as a free person. She saw so many vicious lies and rumors that it made her sick. The other members of the Royal Family tried to see the humor in them but Jennifer found it impossible.

When she flipped to the center page, she was stunned by a picture of a younger Jim Jones. It was a cherubic college pic, but him nonetheless. The headline blazed at her: GOLDEN REIGN OF TERROR. They said his name was Berlin Mansfield and that he was the second most wanted man on earth beside Osama Bin Laden. They went into detail on his escapades alongside General Ratko Mladic in the Serbian War, and how he had double-dealt General Bizimungu and the Hutus throughout the Rwandan War. They said that international bounties on his head were estimated at over a billion dollars, and that he was wanted on suspicion for complicity in terrorist acts across Europe. They conducted an Internet poll and found that he was as hated as Caligula, Attila, Genghis Khan, Hitler, Stalin and Mao. Among his contemporaries, only Bin Laden came close.

She sat in shock for a long time, trying to get her thoughts together. She knew the papers were full of garbage but this was ridiculous. No one could make such things up, not all of them. They said he was a graduate of the University of Berlin, and that was his face. There was some trash talk about him having kidnapped her, but she knew what really happened so that wasn't an issue. There was also something on the cover about her having been kidnapped by aliens, so she wasn't going to get upset over it. The problem she had was this knight in shining armor who she was planning to introduce to the Queen Mother. She anticipated a serious problem here.

What hit her hard was the cult of personality that controlled this 20th century. There were so many stars and celebrities that when it came down to it, there really were none. Most of the people she ran past at the Crown Bar when this started had no idea who she was. She knew who Osama Bin Laden was, but beyond that she had no idea who was on the list after him. Certainly not Jim Jones. If she wore her hat and shades, she could probably go into any department store on Earth with the Queen Mother and they would never be recognized. She was not going to beat herself up for sleeping with Jim Jones, but she sure would find out who Berlin Mansfield was.

She heard the sound of a car approaching and hopped off her chair, rushing to the window and watching Jim get out of the Citroen. She grabbed the tabloid and pulled open the door, coming halfway down the stairs as he walked into the living room.

"Do you think I can speak with you a minute?" she called out, standing with her fists on hips. He blinked at her as the others stared at him before breaking into a chorus of hums, dutifully going back to whatever they had been doing.

"I'll keep the food warm," Sting called as Mansfield followed Jennifer back upstairs.

"I'm sorry I didn't tell you I was stepping out," he began. "I…"

"You know, I've never really had a whole lot of luck picking guys," she said derisively. "Back when I was in school I always ended up with the biggest jerks. My husband was a son of a bitch who cheated on me every chance he got. I'll tell you, though, sometimes you just can't see it coming."

"Was it something I said?"

"What was it you said you did, you said you were a political advisor?"

"That is one of the things I do, but it's…"

"I think things are gonna be pretty slow for you for a while," she slapped the open tabloid onto the table top. "You may wanna write a letter to the editor." Mansfield stared aghast at the expose before him.

"Jennifer, I…"

"Shit!" she stamped her foot at him. "If you weren't Jim Jones you'd be shit!"

"I never knew my father," he turned away, staring out the window in a way that made everything go away but an instinct to comfort him. "He was the King of the Gypsies, an underground prizefighter in Ireland who met my mother at a high-profile affair in Dublin. She was the Duchess of Saxony, and according to what I heard she fell head over heels for him. He was a legend in Ireland, it was nothing for him to be introduced to kings and queens. Only they fell in love, and he traveled back and forth to continue the affair. After she became pregnant, she was targeted by the Baader-Meinhof Gang in Berlin. It was supposed to be a political assassination. They got wrong information and it was my father who was murdered."

"I—I'm sorry," she was taken aback.

"I was sheltered, kept secret from the public. When I found out who and what I was, I withdrew into myself as a recluse. I was sent to schools across Europe so people couldn't make a connection, and I learned how to change who I was. I inherited my father's athletic ability and my mother's analytic mind. I became a star athlete and excelled in chemistry. I had only one goal: revenge against those who wrecked my life. When I graduated from the University, I made connections and joined Baader-Meinhof. It took me a long time but I found the men who killed my father and avenged his death."

"That's terrible," she murmured.

"Only when the Berlin Wall came down and Germany was united, it didn't change things for those who were in the police records. I defected to East Germany but soon I was being hunted across the entire country. By then I had built a reputation for making chemical weapons and I was in demand throughout Europe. I was hired to participate in the Beirut Bombing in 1983, and that was where I established myself. I worked with Hezbollah, Hamas and the PLO for years until I formed my own team and entered the Serbian War in 1991. People kept trying to hire me but I kept raising my prices. They continued to pay, regardless of how ridiculous the price. It's strange, throughout my whole life I had been rejected, the boy nobody wanted. Now here I am, the most wanted man alive."

"Is that supposed to be funny?" she demanded.

"Jennifer, all I wanted to do was to meet you," he poured his heart out. "You captured my imagination, I found you fascinating. I had money, I had connections, I took on the challenge. A friend did me a favor and included me in the Sinn Fein entourage. I had nothing to lose, I asked you for a dance and I thought that was my dream come true. I had no idea you were about to be taken. When I learned what happened I knew I could get you back. The men downstairs are here as a personal favor. None of us have taken money. If we were captured right now, arrangements would be made to have us brought to any one of a dozen countries and executed."

"No," tears began trickling down her cheeks as she stepped towards him. "Never."

"It's why I never said anything when you mentioned me meeting the Queen Mother. I never dreamed of anything coming of this beyond meeting you and kissing your hand. Even though I know once I've returned you to them and may never see you again, I will have my memories. Those they can never ever take away."

He took her into his arms and held her face in his hands, kissing her tears away.

"There will be a way. Maybe you're right, maybe not now, but I won't rest until they acknowledge what you've done. If they're going to forgive the IRA for all they've done for whatever reason, then they should try and forgive you."

"Maybe they won't," he held her close. "But it won't keep me from loving you forever."

He eased her back on his unmade bed, and once again they lost themselves in each other's embrace. They realized that the rest of the gang would be wondering what was going, but they did not care. Mansfield said everything they did not want to admit to themselves, but for now they could only cherish time that they might not ever share again. They drew deeply from each other's nectars and exhausted each other in satisfying their deepest desires at last.

When they finally did rejoin the others, they were relieved to see that they were busy going about their own chores. The others knew they would be going home, the mission over at last. Yet Mansfield knew all too well that things were not always as they seemed, and history had taught them that. Combat was the most unpredictable of man's endeavors, and it could be the slightest unforeseen circumstance that could drive a great victory into the gaping jaws of defeat. One could be vigilant and prepared but it could never be forgotten that anything could happen.

As they departed from the farmhouse on the way to Crossmaglen, Mansfield could not help but remember the setbacks of the past. He remembered the victories in Serbia, the glorious conquests obscured by the massacre at Srebrenica and the subsequent indictments for war crimes by the International Criminal Tribunal. He recalled the rollover victory of the Hutu over the Tutsis, then the war crimes indictments of all concerned, even those who had embezzled and defrauded the regime as had the Mansfield Gang. One never knew what was waiting around the corner, and his fears were realized as he entered the city limits and drove up towards Pat's Pub.

Jon and Slash had driven up a short time earlier and saw the black Mercedes Benz parked out front. The Brits had been inundated by inquiries from international agencies after the operation at Newtownhamilton the night before. As a result they were reluctant to engage in a similar altercation involving demonstrators. They had word that the South Armagh Brigade might be in a position to lend assistance to Mansfield, and sent Jon and Slash to check it out. By now the search for the Princess along the border with the Republic was so intense that Mansfield would have no option but to cross the Irish Sea to make his escape.

The CIA agents were sent to see whether the proprietors of the Pub were planning to help Mansfield along his way.

Slash dropped Jon off at the corner and parked across the intersection, halfway down the block so it would have been nearly impossible to detect his surveillance position. He could see the front of the building, and the partners had agreed that something would come flying through the window as a distress signal. On a quiet Sunday evening after the chaos of the previous night, it was unlikely that such a drastic scenario would arise.

Jon swaggered into Pat's Pub and found the traditional décor of the tavern enhanced by a row of photos along the wall featuring local residents who had served in the Irish Republican Army. He stepped over to inspect the framed pictures and was startled by a gruff voice.

"All right, mate, we're getting' ready t'close for the night."

"Closing?" he turned and faced the bartender and his three hard-faced co-horts sitting at the bar, glaring at Jon. "It's only nine o'clock. Besides, I was expecting somebody."

"We had a casualty at the protest yesterday," the bartender allowed. "He's in hospital, and there's no one to pick 'im up."

"Gee, that's too bad. You think I can get a beer while I call my ride and have 'em pick me up? We were passing through and were planning to do some barhopping around here. This seemed to be like a cool place. Especially with the pictures and all."

"There's a few of these places along the strip out that way, on the West Side," a tall man grunted. "You go on out there you'll see all this kinda stuff."

"Well, how about that beer while I'm waiting?" Jon stepped over and put a twenty-pound note on the bar.

"Okay, but ye'd better call that ride of yers."

Jon asked for a pint of Guinness, pulling out his cell phone to call Slash. The four men continued staring as if to wish him away.

"Hey, bud. Whuzzup? Yeah, this place is closing early, family emergency. What do you think, about a half hour? Okay, see you in a bit."

"Half an hour? Fella, we got an appointment," the bartender insisted.

"Hey whatever happened to Irish hospitality? Look, lemme buy a round here. Get the fellows there a drink, whatever they're having. My guy'll probably be here sooner than that."

"Your guy?" a squat man smirked at the end of the bar. "I thought it was yer mate. Ye mean to tell me ye got somethin' else goin' on there?"

"What are you, kidding?" Jon was annoyed. "It's an expression, you never heard it?"

"We don't want to find out we're drinking with a faggot, boyo," the slender man retorted. "When this fellow shows up, we'd better not see you're lyin' t'us."

Jon was about to shoot off a caustic remark when the door opened, and the five men were caught off-guard by the sight of one of the most beautiful women they had ever seen in Ulster.

"Evening, mate. Can I have a Guinness and a shot of the Mill, then?"

"Sorry, love, it's like I was tellin' this fellow, we're getting ready to close."

"Yeah, well, you were gonna serve me a drink before those feckin' jerks started getting loud back there. Tell you what, why don't you give Smartass' drink to the little lady here."

"I've got my own money, thank you," the woman was curt.

"That's it, close it up," the squat man waved a hand.

"You gonna let that faggot tell you how to run your business?" Jon asked the bartender.

"What's that? Ye callin' me a faggot?"

"Takes one to know one, I figure."

"Oh my God!" the woman cried out.

"All right, that's it!" the bartender roared. "Everybody get the hell out!"

"There's a pair of legs on the floor behind the curtain! Someone's back there and they're not moving!"

"What? Let's see?" Jon came around to where she sat at the head of the bar.

"Okay, everybody stay right where you are," the bartender pulled a pistol and held it at the ready between Jon and the woman. "Let's just stay calm. We're with the RUC, you've just walked into a crime scene. Right now, missus, I need you to walk around to the side of the bar where that fellow's standing. Leave your purse right there, now move it."

"Suppose—someone tries to steal it?"

"That's gonna be the least of your worries if ye don't move it."

"It's probably the owner back there," Jon told the auburn-haired, violet-eyed woman. "These bastards are probably a UDA hit squad."

"Shut yer bleedin' hole, you scum," the bartender cocked the trigger as his associates came up and frisked Jon, pulling his Glock and tossing it atop the bar.

"What's this shite?" the squat man flipped through Jon's wallet. "Universal Exports and Imports? What're you, a smuggler?"

"Better than being a faggot," Jon grinned at him. The man drew his own pistol and pressed the side of it against Jon's face.

"Next remark about fags and I'll blow your balls off so there'll be no more confusion."

"Can you point that thing in a different direction?" the woman pleaded. "If it goes off, it's liable to go right through his head and hit me."

"Aye, and I'm sure there's nothing between his ears to stop it," the squat man cocked his pistol's trigger, sticking the barrel in Jon's ear.

"I thought you said you were gonna blow my balls off," Jon cleared his throat. "You're aiming a little high."

"You know, you're right," the gunman lowered the pistol, pointing it at Jon's groin. "I'd rather you roll around the floor and bleed yerself t'death."

"Say, fellows, I can see I'm interrupting some serious discussion here, so I'd just as soon be on my way and mind my own business," the woman bargained.

"The Mercenaries!" the tall man's eyes widened. "The American Mercenaries! The tabloids mentioned they might be out this way! That's who these two are, I'd bet on it!"

"No, you've got the wrong lass," she started back to collect her purse off the bar. "I'm a citizen of the realm. I'll be on my way then, toodles."

"Stay right where you are or I'll blow your brains out!"

"Sir, you are making a terrible mistake! I've never been to the US in my life!"

"And ye never will if ye don't shut yer hole, ye Fenian bitch!" the bartender bellowed.

"I beg your pardon! I'm a Wiccan!"

Outside the pub, a black SUV was parked down the street facing the front windows in the same exact position as Slash was parked on the other side of the city block. The occupants in the vehicle stared up the street as the man in the front passenger seat set his binoculars aside.

"I see guns in there," Kurt the Bruiser told Berlin Mansfield. "Your contact's been taken out. I suggest we look for a place to lay low until we can get reconnected."

"I agree," Mansfield said as he sat next to the Princess in the back seat. "Yet I tire of all these rats we're finding in the pipeline. Especially after all the help and hospitality we've enjoyed here in South Armagh. Kurt, why not blow those fellows a kiss goodbye?"

"Yeah, what the hell," Kurt agreed. "Sting, go on and get me a launcher."

"Just the vehicle, not the building," Mansfield insisted.

"What are you doing!" Jennifer was alarmed.

"*He* ain't doing squat," Chopper chuckled along with the others. "He just takes the credit."

"Thank God," Sting cackled before he exited the van and darted to the hatchback.

"We're sending a message," Mansfield reassured Jennifer. "I'm quite sure someone has double-crossed the people who were going to help us cross the sea to England."

The battle-tested team was in position in the blink of an eye, and Sting was already returning the RPG-7 to the hatchback as the vehicle in front of the pub exploded in a ball of flames. They would not be able to see the window glass shattering from the blast, or the people inside the pub diving for cover as the shards were blown like wind-swept hail.

Jon Stevens, like the Mansfield Gang, had experienced the savagery of war in Serbia and lived through his share of shellfire. Most were of the opinion that, though cover was the best way to avoid shrapnel injury, if a hit was a hit there was nothing one could do about it. It provided for Jon to lunge for one of the loose pistols on the floor, then roll to his feet as he got the drop on the UDA assassins.

"Okay, you bastards, now it's your move," he waved the gun between them as the woman scrambled to her feet.

"Can I get my purse?"

"Go right ahead. Go behind the bar, draw me a Guinness and leave your name and number on a piece of paper."

"Are you gonna call me?"

"If I make it through the night, you bet I will."

Berlin Mansfield always knew that it was the fickle finger of fate that decided the fortunes of men. It brought the authorities at the most inopportune time, spelling doom for the armed robber, the cat burglar, the peeping tom, and even the drunkard pissing in the street. In this case it was a recon helicopter soaring above the clouds, roaming aimlessly until the explosion below caught their attention. They noted an SUV roaring down the highway, reporting the vehicle before descending to call ground support to the scene.

Slash Scimitar parked the BMW peripherally on the street corner at a safe distance to the flaming vehicle, rushing inside the pub with his gun drawn to back Jon up. Within minutes the RUC squad cars surrounded the property, the officers rushing the building with their weapons at the ready. Jon and Slash escorted the woman named Celeste out of the pub as the police took control of the situation.

"One of our helicopters picked up a black Citroen speeding along the A37 towards Dundalk," Mark reported as Jon checked in on his cell phone. "I'll let you do the honors, but remember, we want this over and done with. If we can't take them without a fight then we'll turn it over to the local police. They're cornered, there's no way out."

Father George Sohn was praying for the people of South Armagh before finally blowing out the candles in the chapel, blissfully unaware of the latest sectarian confrontation in the neighboring city. The other four parish priests were away for the weekend tending to friends, family and relatives in nearby Armagh. He had stayed behind to tend to the rectory and maintain a prayer vigil for the victims of the violence. He prayed they might get back to where they were before the Princess of Edinburgh was kidnapped, ever so close to a peace treaty at long last.

He was going to call it a night when he heard a knock on the chapel door. He was immediately alarmed as it was far too late for anyone arriving for services. Yet his code of ethics required him to remain available for those in need regardless of circumstances. He could only pray that it was not a hate group attempting to launch an attack on the Church. In that case he could only place his fate in God's hands.

He opened the door and was surprised at two men wearing black hoodies at the door.

"Greetings, Father. I am Father Jones and this is Father Kurt. We were traveling around the Continent and decided to stop here in Ireland. We crossed the border after visiting Dublin and encountered a civil disturbance in Armagh. We hoped to take a ferry to England in the morning but have no place to spend the evening. Perhaps we might be able to rest here in the chapel until sunrise."

"How many of you are there?"

"There are seven of us. Six priests and a Sister of Charity."

"Why, certainly. As a matter of fact, the other fathers here are traveling this weekend. You'd be welcome to use their rooms."

"Wonderful. I'll let them know."

Father George walked to the heavy wooden door of the chapel and watched as the other black-clad figures approached the chapel. Father Jones introduced them all as they walked in carrying heavy duffel bags, but the Sister of Charity caused him to do a double-take.

"This is Sister Jennifer," Father Jones peered from beneath his black hood.

"You—you're the Princess of Edinburgh! Your picture is all over the telly!"

"She gets that all the time," Father Jones assured him.

"C'mon, Boss, he may be dumb but he's not blind," Kurt the Bruiser grunted, pulling off his hoodie to reveal his tattooed 22" biceps accentuated by his sleeveless black T-shirt. "Let's see if we can get some chow and some z's before we find us a boat ride."

"I suppose so," Mansfield replied, pulling off his gray wig and tossing it at Father George, revealing his graying black mane and smoldering cobalt eyes. "My companions are hungry. We are escorting the Princess back to London and would like to refresh ourselves for the trip. The Protestants are very much against us, I'm sure you can appreciate that."

"Of course, of course," Father George nearly dropped the wig in a fright. At first he thought the man had scalped himself. "There are some provisions in the Frigidaire, I'll make you a meal."

"God bless you, Father," Mansfield clapped his shoulders.

Father George made his way to the kitchen, intimidated by the menacing aura of his visitors. There was the sociopathic Chopper, the shifty-eyed Van Tran, the cold-eyed Cat and the arrogant Sting. He was somewhat comforted by the presence of the Princess who followed to help him in the kitchen. Yet he cringed at the thought of Father Jones being Berlin Mansfield, who was said to be the Devil himself.

"My Princess," Father George managed as the Princess took off her hoodie, wearing her black T-shirt to help him with the cooking. "How long have you been free? The entire country of Northern Ireland is looking for you."

"I was rescued Saturday night," she revealed. "We tried to escape through Newtownhamilton but there was rioting and we had to return to the place we were staying. We drove through Crossmaglen a couple of hours ago but we came across another terror attack. There has been violence in every direction we've turned. I simply must get back to try and put an end to all this."

"That fellow—the man traveling with you," the priest hesitated. "Is that— Berlin Mansfield?"

"No, that's Jim," she smiled sweetly. "I met Jim Jones at the dance, the night I was kidnapped. Jim is the man who rescued me."

Father George considered all these things as he set about making a huge pan of Ulster fry. He knew that the forces of evil had kidnapped the Princess to derail the peace negotiations. Yet he may have been the only person in Northern Ireland to know that she may have been delivered unto a greater evil. If this was indeed Berlin Mansfield, then he may well be holding the Princess for an even greater demand than anyone could fathom. He prayed mightily that God would intercede and save the Princess from the horror that might well loom ahead.

His heart leapt for joy as he heard a pounding on the chapel door once again. He only hoped it was none of the other priests of the parish returning, lest they panic at the sight of the strangers and make a move that might provoke violence. He prayed that it was the authorities conducting a random patrol of the area and come to see that all was well. They could take custody of the Princess and return her to Buckingham Palace where she could complete her historical mission in bringing peace to Northern Ireland.

The gangsters waited for Father George to come down to the chapel and answer the door. He could hear the sound of metal clattering in the shadows and felt a chill down his spine. He feared the worst and only wished the Princess had not followed him from the kitchen in the rectory through the passageway to the chapel. He prayed to the Blessed Virgin that there be no bloodshed and that the suffering of the people of Ulster come to an end at last.

"Greetings, friends. How can I help you?"

"Good evening," the auburn-haired man in black stood at the threshold with his companion as the six men inside the chapel gathered around in curiosity. "I'm Father Stevens and this is Father Slash. We were in the area and can really use a place to stay for the night. I saw the car parked outside and I thought maybe you were providing shelter for travelers here."

"This place is full," Kurt the Bruiser was belligerent. "Try the church down the street."

"Hey, bro," Slash Scimitar spotted Sting Ramipril in the crowd around the door. "You look like you're a long way from home. You wouldn't be from that swampland in Jamaica."

"The only swamps I ever crossed was bringing Jamaican rum to the beggars in Grenada."

Jon Stevens rolled his eyes, knowing what was coming next.

* * *

Prove to me you are the new day
My sunrise swollen with singing birds
Breeze my elixir, flowers my fairies
Caressing the dawn as the day
And lest we forget our love
The butterflies remind us as ever
There's something that sparkled
floated in those moments
Don't let me think of you gone
Not just departed for a moment
not that moment
You held me in your arms and I felt
The springtime shrouded around me
And I knew rebirth, life, love
Yet I wonder now what I knew
So prove to me you are the new day
Turn your magic moonlight
To the sparkle of twilight
Be my new day.

* * *

Mansfield and Jennifer fell into each other's arms, realizing that this might be their farewell kiss. They tasted each other's lips, wanting to be able to always remember this magic moment. He eased her away towards Father George, who grabbed her as Mansfield drew his weapon along with the others. They began firing at the doorway as they raced down the aisle, Mansfield cutting to the left towards the stairwell leading to the upper balcony. His five teammates dispersed by the altar as Chuck and Benny ran into the sacristy, while Kurt, Al and Sting ducked into the front pew to provide cover fire.

The shots alerted the RUC patrol nearby, who radioed O'Shaughnessy's SAS squad in an Apache helicopter above the clouds. The chopper descended above the chapel so that O'Shaughnessy and his eleven teammates could lower themselves by rope onto the roof. O'Shaughnessy was the first to land, and he immediately secured a rappelling line to a sturdy smokestack. He then dropped the line over the side and lowered himself to one of the stained glass windows. He kicked the glass in and pulled himself inside as the gunfire echoed from the lower level of the chapel.

Jon and Slash rolled through the doorway, taking cover behind the back row as they returned fire. Jon saw Mansfield run to the stairwell and followed in pursuit as Slash began moving to his right where he saw Sting scurrying off. Kurt began moving towards the opposite row of benches to ambush Jon while Al followed to take his place. Slash popped up and shot Al in the right hip before tumbling as Sting emptied his clip at his position.

"Come on," Jennifer insisted as she and Father George crouched in the pew across from where Slash began crawling up the aisle along the east wall. "I've got to get you out of here."

"Give me your confession, my child," he gazed into her eyes. "I doubt we will have a chance for anything else."

"Let me tell you something," she said intently. "I've been kidnapped for over two weeks, I've had one decent bath since, my hair's a mess and my feet are all blistered. I don't want to have to drag a man out a door under gunfire to top it off."

"I beg your pardon?"

"All right then, let's go!"

Jennifer and Father George fled out the front door just as Benny Van Tran and Chuck Chop ran out the back exit. Chuck hopped behind a short wall near a small garden, then watched quizzically as Benny headed for the Citroen parked near the back fence.

"Give me the key," Benny insisted, Mansfield having given it to Chuck as had been preplanned.

"What, are you nuts?" Chuck snarled back, training his gun on the rear door of the chapel. "The guys're coming out this way. They won't know where the hell we are!"

"Look over the roof," Benny motioned with his Glock before pointing it at Chuck. "That's a military helicopter. Wake up and smell the coffee. This place will be surrounded if it's not already. Mansfield doesn't have it anymore. He put us together to go rescue that broad so he could get laid and we don't make a dime. We don't lose shit without him. We can make contact with the General in Rwanda and get a new deal going without him for twice what we made last time. C'mon, Chuck, gimme the keys so we can get outta here."

"Are you outta your fuggin' mind?" Chuck looked back before Benny fired a shot into the back of his neck just above his flak jacket. Benny ran over, pulled the keys from Chuck's pants pocket, then returned to the Citroen and hopped in. He gunned the engine and sailed down the country road on the way to the Dundalk harbor.

Kurt saw Jon run into the stairwell in pursuit of Mansfield and chased after him. He was entirely unaware of O'Shaughnessy watching from the balcony. Mark ran around to the upper stairwell, but instead of making a move to intercept Mansfield, he climbed over the balcony rail. He swung out over the aisle along the west wall and hurtled himself at Kurt, his full 300-pound weight crashing elbow first onto Kurt's neck. The Bruiser crashed to the floor, then turned to his attacker and rose with blood in his eyes. Mark O'Shaughnessy realized he was going to be in for the fight of his life.

Slash rushed Sting just as he was reloading his Glock, tackling the Jamaican across the floor. Sting caught Slash on the way in and monkey-flipped him across the floor. The two men leaped to their feet and squared off against one another.

"Well, you ugly bastard," Sting sneered, "just the fellow I wanted to talk to."

"You won't be doing too much talking after I kick your teeth down your throat," Slash snarled back. They locked up as a pair of praying mantises doing battle, their long limbs entwining around their opponent's as they tumbled to the floor. They were trying to choke each other out but were having trouble getting their hands past the other's long, sinewy arms.

"Mansfield!" Jon yelled up the stairs to the upper level, holding his Glock at the ready as he peered past the steel post along the handrail. "The place is surrounded! They've got police and Army units on the way! Throw down your gun and I'll walk you out of here!"

Jon hissed as a slug ricocheted off the post right next to his face, smashing into the wall behind him and sending a spray of plaster chips across the steps. He lunged out and began firing at the next flight of steps, watching Mansfield's boot disappear just as the bullets hammered into the wall where he had stood a microsecond ago. Jon held his gun at the ready as he tiptoed up the steps, taking them two at a time. He knew that Mansfield would be trapped on the upper balcony and would probably try to fight it out here instead.

He tensed himself at the next landing, realizing he might get one shot off before Mansfield returned fire. If Mansfield escaped out onto the balcony, Jon would merely have to guard the doorway to make sure he did not try running back to the stairwell. He could hear the sirens in the distance outside and knew it was just about over.

Jon coiled himself like a steel spring before pouncing out into the open. He emptied his clip at the figure on the next landing, and Mansfield's eyes were wide with amazement as the bullets caught him square in the chest. Jon watched as he was thrown backwards by the force which catapulted him backwards through the stained glass window into the darkness.

Jennifer and Father George made it to the front gate before they were dragged to the ground by two SAS commandos, who covered their mouths as they announced themselves. Once the two stopped struggling, the commandos pulled them to their feet and led them down the path through the front gate where police vans were surrounding the property line.

"Are you the Princess?" a commando asked.

"Yes," Jennifer replied. "Tell them not to shoot, there's innocent people inside!"

"We've got it taken care of, milady," he replied. "Let me get you and the priest back to our command vehicle. You're safe now, it's over."

Benny Van Tran raced the Citroen up the road but slammed on the brakes as he saw a flaming blockade on the path before him. He started to back up but saw a figure pounce up onto the hood of the car as rifle barrels smashed through the windows on either side of the front seat.

"Turn off the car or we'll blow your head off!" a rifleman yelled as the man on the hood smashed the windshield with a crowbar. He stared into the rear view mirror and saw riflemen's laser sights beaming into his eyes. He turned the van off, realizing it was over at last.

Not even Berlin Mansfield could get out of this mess.

On both sides of the chapel, the SAS commandos had lowered themselves in front of the windows. They crashed in at once, rolling and tumbling over the pews and exploding into action. They pried the West Indians apart on the east aisle and cuffed Sting face down on the floor. Along the west aisle, they pulled Mark and Kurt away from each other after the Bruiser had nearly dropped O'Shaughnessy with a crushing right cross to the jaw.

"We've got him, sir," a commando hugged Mark's shoulders as the others pulled Kurt up after cuffing his wrists behind his back.

"That's the toughest son of a bitch I've ever fought," Mark was handed a handkerchief with which he wiped blood from a gash in his eyebrow, then patted the steady trickle from his nose. He cried out as he forced his broken nose back into place before throwing a hard right that nearly dropped the Bruiser from the arms of his captors.

"You've got a thing about getting in the last lick," Jon shook his head as he came over to the SAS commandos. "You want to send your guys outside to pick up Mansfield. I put five slugs dead center in him. He went out the window into the churchyard."

"You heard him," Mark ordered an SAS sergeant. "Go out and get him bagged and tagged. Take the rest of these bastards out front, hand them over to the UDR. I want armored trucks escorting them every meter of the way back to the navy yard."

"I sure taught that Jamaican bastard something about fighting Grenadans," Slash rubbed his bleeding knuckles.

"You fellows can take the ride back with us on the chopper," Mark decided. "The Princess will be taken back under armed guard in one of the vans. I think she's had enough excitement for one lifetime."

"Sir," a UDR rifleman came over to where the three men stood. "We've got floodlights all over the property and four squads of men out there. There's no sign of Mansfield anywhere."

"Bullshit!" Jon was astonished. "That clip was loaded with Teflon-coated shells. Even if he was wearing a bullet-proof vest, it would've taken him out."

Mark stormed out the door with the CIA agents behind him, and it was if a movie were being made at the chapel. Military trucks mounted with spotlights were on all sides of the property, shining their beams across the building and the surrounding grounds. The troops and police officers searched every inch of the landscape, particularly outside the window through which Mansfield had fallen.

The Golden Terror was nowhere to be found.

Jennifer had insisted that she be taken by helicopter back to South Armagh despite the protests of the military officers on site. She assured them that she would file a formal complaint if her wishes were not granted. They loaded her onto another Apache on site and flew her back to Newtownhamilton, radioing ahead so that a force of considerable size would be awaiting them. Within the half hour they were descending into the conflict-weary city, the Apache landing in a soccer field outside the downtown area where she was taken to an armed convoy.

Shannon Blackburn had extended her stay after the conflagration of the previous night. More and more Catholics and Protestants were converging at the rally and sharing the hospitality of the Princess Search team and their new-found cattle market sponsors. It had turned into a block party of sorts, almost in defiance of the authorities that had converged on the neighborhood and hammered it into submission. They would show that they were not only loyal citizens, but they would not give up their rights and liberties their country guaranteed them.

She had read a statement from Deryl Lee Kilmarnoch thanking both communities for their support, and encouraging them to continue joining together as a united people in this United Kingdom. He assured them that their prayers and brotherhood would bring the blessing of God to their country, quoting from the Book of Ecclesiastes in guaranteeing their land would be healed. There were over a thousand people surrounding the stage that had been erected, and they clapped and cheered as Shannon finished her presentation. She was on her way off the stage when she stopped at the sound of a familiar voice over the sound system.

"Hold on, Shannon. I think you can close it down for the night."

She whirled around and was as astounded as everyone else at the sight of Jennifer Mac Manus walking onstage with a wireless microphone. She rushed over and the two women embraced each other as the huge crowd went wild with excitement.

The Princess Search was over at last.

Chapter Ten

The return of the Princess of Edinburgh to Buckingham Palace was an event that brought the attention of the world press to the United Kingdom. It immediately turned into a segue for the historic event. Loyalists and Republicans met with British diplomats at Stormont Castle to sign the Good Friday Agreement of 1998. Jennifer was hospitalized with nervous exhaustion upon returning to England but checked herself out early to attend the signing.

More than anything, she wanted to understand what had happened and what triggered the chain of events. She knew that she would have to withdraw from the process if she believed there was a guilty party, and it was far too late for that. Yet she had not seen a face of evil. There was no one out there who was dead set on killing others for no reason. She knew that there were men in Maghaberry Prison serving life sentences for serial killings and mass murder, but these were not the men leading the struggle. There would always be murderers in society. Yet times like these allowing the chance to redeem a society came once in a lifetime.

She found that Baxter Cody and his squad had planned the entire operation in a righteous attempt to derail what he believed was a process that would lead to the secession of Ulster from the United Kingdom. MI6 had determined that Cody had submitted detailed plans, risk assessments, evaluations and projected gains and losses that might be incurred as a result of the action. All of these had been ignored and ridiculed by his superior, UDA Brigadier Ed Doherty. Cody construed the Brigade's failure to commit as tacit approval, and went through with the abduction before they realized what was happening.

Jennifer also learned that the UDA was a militant group formed as a bulwark against the IRA, but had allowed gangsterism to obscure their vision.

They resorted to drug trafficking to fund their paramilitary operations, and soon turned their network into a multimillion-pound criminal empire. Many of the Old Guard were soured by the way the young guns were impacting the organization with their racketeering schemes, and Cody was an anachronism in that regard. He believed in a political victory ensured by armed force, while Ed Doherty had lost his way through the river of money flowing through his territory. The clash of ideologies resulted in Jennifer being spared and Doherty sacrificed in the Armagh warehouse.

She was finally able to see how the IRA had become the sympathetic figure in this passion play. The Catholic minority was being hammered from pillar to post with only the IRA to turn to. The Provos, in turn, were following an obscure socialist policy dictated from Dublin, which might as well have come from another world. The IRA leadership in the Republic had fallen victim to the same greed that had corrupted the UDA infrastructure. One of the greatest paradoxes in the conflict was that the same paramilitary that supported the Evil Mothers was funded by a multimillion-dollar drug racket in the Irish capitol.

An even greater irony came in the form of Shannon Blackburn's appointment as the Sinn Fein County Adjutant in Armagh. The Republicans saw the magnetism of the leader of Princess Search and made an offer in hopes of riding the crest of her budding popularity. The UDA in Belfast was astonished by the development but decided to cut their losses. Jennifer learned that Shannon had been an assassin for the Doherty mob. It was only by Royal Decree that Jennifer was given access to the top secret MI6 documents on Shannon's past. The one thing that stuck out in Jennifer's mind was an interrogator commenting that interviewing Shannon was like having a conversation with the Devil himself.

Of all the characters in this strange and surreal drama, it was O'Shaughnessy she was afraid of. He represented the 21st century just around the corner, the technological terror that Orwell had written about. Once again governments had replaced the gods, and now they could see into the secret places of men and hear their most intimate conversations. If, as it was said, they could see a mosquito on a horse's ass from Chernobyl, then what would stop them from looking into the home of every citizen of the UK? What would stop them from falling into the ultimate temptation of keeping files on every person on earth? Where would liberty end and security begin? How could the government ensure there would always be something that could stop people like O'Shaughnessy from always getting their man by any means necessary?

She also found that Jon Stevens and Osborne 'Slash' Scimitar were CIA agents who had been assigned to surveillance in front of the Hotel Europa on the night she was kidnapped. Jon had been her guardian angel every step of the way, nearly freeing her at Port Muck, coming in a half hour late at both Londonderry and Armagh. It was he who had forced Berlin's hand at Dundalk, and he who had nearly taken Berlin's life. Yet it was he who had been there from start to finish, and it was he who she owed this last dance.

The celebration at the Hotel Europa was as Christmas and New Year's rolled into one as the world press and emissaries from dozens of nations came to Belfast for the historic occasion. It seemed as if the entire British Army had turned out as well to ensure that this event would not be marred as the last. Once again the food and entertainment were second to none, and everyone was dressed as if for the Academy Awards as they arrived to share in the festivities.

"I guess I can die a happy man," Jon Stevens kissed Jennifer's hand as he escorted her back to the dais after their dance at the ceremonial banquet. "It's not every day you get to dance with a beautiful Princess."

"Thank you for saving me," she looked into his eyes. "I'll never forget what you did. You were the first to see me go and the first to bring me back."

"You're a beautiful girl, Princess," he smiled. "If you weren't married to England I'd grab you in a second."

"You know my address," she squeezed his hands in hers. "Anytime you're in town you give me a call, and I mean it. I'll jump into some jeans and we'll go for a pint. I'm just Jennifer to you. If you come through and don't call I'll be hurt."

"Your wish is my command...Jennifer," he kissed her hand again before returning to his place of honor at the front table, causing her heart to skip a beat. Dressed in a $1,000 tuxedo, he certainly fit the image as a knight in shining attire.

"Excuse me, milady," one of the chief stewards came over to her as she took her seat at the dais alongside other dignitaries of the UK. "You have a private call on the chef's line. They said it was an important personal matter."

At once she felt a wave of panic, a feeling of helplessness in knowing *they* were still out there. The UDA, the IRA, the PLO, Hezbollah, Hamas, Osama Bin Laden...all lurking somewhere in the shadows. Perhaps she feared what Mark O'Shaughnessy represented, but he would argue that after all was said and done, he was the only thing that kept her safe from the demons of the night. She wished desperately that he would be there beside her when she took this call, that he would be beside her every step of the way back to Buckingham Palace. Only she knew when she woke up the next day she would curse herself for her weakness.

Still there was Jon Stevens and Slash Scimitar, both of whom were decorated by the Queen in a secret ceremony due to the clandestine nature of their operations. They were here, and so were the six-foot-six giants who followed at a respectful distance, dressed in suits which concealed holstered weapons appearing as mini-cannons. There were still "Knights of the Round Table" in England's dreaming, those who lived to protect and to serve. There were those who would sacrifice themselves to save a lost child as quickly as the Princess of Edinburgh. It made her feel a lot better as she approached the nervous-looking wait staff members who escorted her to the phone.

"Hello?"

"Jennifer."

She nearly dropped the receiver before catching her breath and distancing herself into a corner of the room.

"Oh my god. Where are you?"

"Somewhere far and away from Mark O'Shaughnessy and his pesky snoops. If he's listening, I'm sure he'll be sorely disappointed."

"I don't care who's listening. Are you okay? They said they were sure you were killed and someone took your body away."

"They said the same thing about our Lord Jesus Christ, unfortunately for them. He lives forever, and so do I. In your heart, I hope. As long as I live, you will be in mine."

"You know," she fought to keep from crying.

"I am the sun's reflection on the lake, I am the breeze rustling the trees. I'm with the birds flying across the sky, I'm with the children playing. I'm in the scent of the hyacinth whose fragrance is carried by the wind and fills your bosom. Wherever you see, hear, taste or breathe these things, remember I am there with you."

"I know," tears spilled down her cheeks.

"I'll call again, and one day when they forget us we will meet again. I'll love you until it is more than I can bear, and then I will come to you to take my pain away. I'll dream of your kisses, your beautiful eyes, the scent of your hair, in my dreams, forever and ever."

"Berlin…"

"Jennifer."

The line went dead.

She held the receiver against her heart for a long time, and finally returned it to its cradle as the mystified wait staff looked on. She wiped her eyes and wandered down to the end of the hallway as the giants remained at a watchful distance. She didn't care if Mark O'Shaughnessy or the whole world was listening. She would love Berlin Mansfield until the day she died, and no matter what they said or did, nothing could steal that love away from her.

She looked out the window into the starry sky, and smiled in knowing Berlin had forgotten one thing.

He was in the moonlight too.

Lightning Source UK Ltd.
Milton Keynes UK
UKHW041932200121
377415UK00009B/488/J